THE GUNSMITH

#20

THE DODGE CITY GANG

Other Books
By
J.R. Roberts

THE GUNSMITH

#20

THE DODGE CITY GANG

J.R. ROBERTS

SPEAKING VOLUMES, LLC
NAPLES, FLORIDA
2013

THE GUNSMITH
#20 THE DODGE CITY GANG

ISBN 978-1-61232-623-8

To the Dodge City Gang:

Charlie Bassett

Bill Tilghman

Ben Thompson

Bat Masterson

Ed Masterson

Wyatt Earp

Neal Brown

Without them there would have been no story.

Chapter One

A mile outside of Dodge City, Kansas, the rattler was sunning itself on a large rock, and the sandy color of the reptile's skin caused it to blend into the stone as if they were one and the same.

If the Gunsmith's horse Duke had merely been an ordinary animal, their meeting with the snake might have been catastrophic. Duke's excellent instincts for survival, however, successfully separated the snake from the stone, and warned Clint Adams in plenty of time. They had already spotted the reptile when suddenly it reared up, showed its fangs and began to transmit its message of death with the rattle on its tail.

"Okay, Duke, I see him," Clint assured the big black gelding.

It would have been a simple thing for the Gunsmith to draw his gun and shoot off the snake's head—or even his rattler—and for a moment Clint considered it, but then he

1

changed his mind. It was just as easy to give the creature a wide berth and allow it to continue sunning itself on the rock.

Duke began to fidget, eager to put some distance between himself and the snake, and Clint jerked on the reins and said, "Okay, big fella, we're going."

He directed the big gelding in a wide circle around the snake, and then back on to the road to Dodge City, where his friend Bat Masterson was waiting for him—at least, that was what the telegram said. He'd find out for sure when he got there. He had left his team and rig in Labyrinth, Texas for safekeeping, and had ridden most of the night to get to Dodge City. Bat had made it sound vital that he reach Dodge as soon as possible.

Clint had never been to Dodge himself, but he knew it was a wide-open town, and he had been in towns *like* that before, most notably Abilene, Kansas,* where he had served as a deputy under his friend Wild Bill Hickok.

He hadn't seen Bat since they had put on a boxing tournament together in Willow Falls, Arizona.† That had been Bat's idea, and it had ended up being something of a mess. Clint wondered what kind of a mess Bat had gotten himself into this time. He had first met Masterson through Wyatt Earp, back in Caldwell, Kansas,†† when all of them had gotten into a jam together. It seemed like whenever two or three of them got together, trouble happened. If past history was any indication, he was heading right straight for it again—which wasn't unusual for the man they called the Gunsmith

But if Clint had known what he was really heading into,

* *The Gunsmith #4: The Guns of Abilene*
† *The Gunsmith #9: Heavyweight Gun*
††*The Gunsmith #5: Three Guns for Glory*

he might have looked at that rattler as an omen. And he would have known that the snake was the least dangerous thing he'd run into during the coming week.

Chapter Two

Charlie Bassett was the sheriff of Ford County, Kansas, where Dodge City was located, but the real reason that Dodge was almost well in hand were his two deputies, Bill Tilghman and Bat Masterson. Tilghman had come first, and the news of his appointment was met with laughter and more than a few winking eyes, because he was barely twenty-one at the time, and the Dodge City toughs thought he'd be easy.

They were more than wrong.

The gamblers and cowboys of Dodge decided to test the young deputy, and picked a man named Texas Bill to do it.

Tilghman was standing in front of the Alhambra saloon one night when Texas Bill crossed his path with two friends, all of them wearing guns.

"You'll have to turn your guns in, boys," Bill informed them. "New town ordinance."

"I never heard of it," Texas Bill said. "If you want my guns, sonny, you'll have to come and get them."

Now Texas Bill was a fair hand with a gun, and what happened next was talked about in Dodge for a long time to come.

When Bill moved, Texas Bill assumed the lawman was going for his gun, and he did the same, only Bill Tilghman's lightning quick hands never went anywhere near his gun.

As Texas Bill's hand streaked for his gun, Bill Tilghman's fists lashed out faster than the eye could see, and suddenly the burly gunman was toppling forward, out cold. His two friends exchanged glances, but as they moved they were also met by Tilghman's pistonlike fists and after catching several blows each in the stomach, they fell to the ground, where they were when Bill removed all of their guns.

"The jail's that way, boys," Bill Tilghman told them, "and it looks like you're going to get a long look at the inside. Pick up your friend and let's go."

Front Street couldn't believe what had happened, but it wasn't too long before the people of Dodge decided to comply with the no-guns ordinance. There were, however, a handful of Texans who resented Tilghman, and one of them was a young gunhawk name Clay Allison, who already had an awesome reputation with a gun. He said that he'd gun Tilghman down before he could get close enough to use his fists.

Tilghman had heard the talk, and was waiting for the day Allison came to town to try it.

Soon after that, twenty-one-year-old Bat Masterson came to town, and Charlie Bassett signed him up as a deputy as well. Between the three of them—most notably the two young deputies—they were able to keep the lid on Dodge City in a way that had not been done in years.

Bat Masterson's telegram had gone out to Clint Adams after the Alhambra's owner, Mayor "Dog" Kelly, had gotten word that the largest number of Texas cowboys in history were heading for Dodge, and the saloon keeper was afraid that the two young lawmen—as good as they obviously were—might not be able to handle them.

Kelly decided to send for some people to help Masterson and Tilghman out, but Bat decided to send for someone on his own.

The Gunsmith.

When Clint rode into Dodge, it didn't look quite like the wide-open town he had heard about, but then it was still early in the day, and towns like Dodge and Abilene had a way of blossoming at night.

He put Duke up at the livery, paying extra to assure that the big gelding was well taken care of, then went in search of a hotel and a drink. Once he was registered at the hotel, he went straight to the Alhambra saloon, figuring that sooner or later Bat Masterson would find his way there for a drink, a woman, a poker game, or all three.

"What can I get you?" the bartender asked.

"A beer, thanks," Clint said. He turned his back on the bar and looked over the Alhambra's impressive setup. It was reminiscent of the Alamo saloon in Abilene, which brought back some painful memories of Bill Hickok and the way he'd been killed, which Clint tried to shake off.

He picked up his beer and took a look around the room at all the gaming tables—poker, roulette, faro—but Bat Masterson was not yet in evidence. In fact, the tables were still fairly empty.

"I'd heard this was a hell of a wide-open town," Clint said, turning back to the bartender.

"Give it a few hours, friend," the man answered. "Even Dodge City gotta sleep sometime."

"I guess. Do you know Bat Masterson?"

"Deputy sheriff."

"Has he been around today?"

"Nope. You need something from the law, maybe you better talk to Sheriff Charlie Bassett or the other deputy, Bill Tilghman. Him and Bat are pretty good friends."

"Where can I find Tilghman?"

"Stick around. Tilghman'll be in before long. You a friend of Masterson's?"

"That's right." When the man didn't say anything else, Clint said, "Why did you ask?"

The bartender shrugged and said, "Those two boys are gonna need all the friends they can get, that's all."

"Why?"

"Trouble's coming," the barkeep said, "and it's riding hard."

"That's the only way it does ride. Can you tell me anything else?"

"All I know is that trouble is coming," the man said again. He glanced down the bar and said, "I got other customers to take care of."

Clint sipped his beer. Bat wouldn't have sent for him if trouble wasn't coming, he guessed he'd known that right off, but now it was confirmed.

Clint finished his beer and decided to take a walk over to the jail and present himself to Sheriff Bassett. It was a custom he followed in every town he visited anyway, and for now he'd keep it to himself that he was in town in answer to a telegram from Bat.

It would have been just as easy for the Gunsmith to mount up and ride out of Dodge and avoid that hard-riding trouble, but Bat was his friend, and there weren't all that many men he could say that about. Riding out never crossed Clint Adams's mind. It might have been the smart thing to do, but it wouldn't have been the right thing to do.

Not to a friend.

Chapter Three

"Sheriff Bassett?" Clint asked the man behind the desk in the sheriff's office.

"That's right," the man answered. He was in his mid-forties, with sandy hair that was going gray, and an exceptionally large nose that seemed to dwarf his other features. "What can I do for you?"

"My name is Clint Adams," the Gunsmith said, and then paused to see if the name would mean anything to the lawman. It obviously did. "I'm just checking in," Clint told the lawman, "to let you know that I'm in your town."

"That's right nice of you, Mr. Adams," Bassett said. "How long would you be planning to stay?"

"I haven't decided that yet."

"What brings you to Dodge?"

"A friend of mine lives here. One of your deputies, Bat Masterson," Clint explained.

"Bat's out of town now, but he should be back tomorrow."

"Then I'll be here at least until then, Sheriff."

"That's fine. Have you got a room yet?"

"Yes, at the Dodge House."

"It's a good hotel, with good food."

"Glad to hear it."

"Thanks for stopping by, Mr. Adams. I wish all our guests were as helpful."

"Well, being an exlawman myself, I try to be as helpful to the law as I can."

"I appreciate that," Bassett said, standing up and putting out his hand. "It was a pleasure to meet you."

"Thanks," Clint said, shaking the man's hand. "If you see Bat before I do, you'll tell him I'm in town, won't you?"

"I sure will."

"Thanks."

Clint decided to head over to the hotel for lunch. When he arrived at the dining room he had a pleasant surprise. There were two waitresses working the room. One was in her forties, thin and plain looking. The other one was not much younger, but there the similarity stopped. Clint spotted her as soon as he sat down, and he could see that she had also spotted him. When the other waitress approached to take his order, the better looking one stopped her, said something to her, and then came over to Clint's table.

Up close he could see that she was in her late thirties, but there was a quality about her, an earthiness that reached out and grabbed him, tightening his groin. She was blond and blue eyed, and her uniform and eyes were filled with a ripe promise.

"What can I get for you, stranger?" she asked, catching his eyes and holding them tight.

"What's your specialty?" Clint asked her.

Her full lips spread into a wide smile and she said, "Something that ain't on the menu . . ."

". . . but we can discuss that another time, right?"

"That's right."

They understood each other perfectly, and times like that between a man and a woman were rare.

"Why don't you bring me a lot of food," he told her. "I'll trust your judgment."

She raised her eyebrows and said, "So will I. Would you like a drink while you wait, or is it too early?"

"A cold beer would be nice."

"Coming up," she said. She lingered a moment, wetting her lips while she studied his face, then turned and went to the kitchen while Clint eyed her full, swaying hips.

His stay in Dodge was starting to show some promise.

During lunch Clint introduced himself to the comely waitress, whose name turned out to be Maggie Lane, and by the time she brought him his coffee, they were friends. Not knowing what Bat had in store for him, however, Clint refrained from asking the woman to have dinner with him just yet. That could always come later, after he spoke with Bat. Besides, his all-night ride, which now appeared to have been unnecessary, since Bat hadn't been there to greet him, was beginning to take its toll. For once the Gunsmith was thinking about bed in terms of a nap, and not a woman.

That condition was destined to be short-lived, however. No sooner had Clint lain down on the bed in his hotel room, than there was a knock at the door. Reluctantly and with his usual caution, he opened the door.

It was Maggie, the waitress. "I figured maybe you were a little shy and didn't want to ask me up here right away."

"Oh?"

"And since you're a stranger in town, and probably just passing through, I decided to be a little bold." She paused, and then said, "Is that all right?"

"That's fine," he told her, then took her by the shoulders and drew her into the room, saying, "That's just fine, but I think I should warn you."

"About what?"

"I may be in town a few days longer than you think."

She thought that over, then said, "I'll tell you afterward whether that's fine with me or not. Okay?"

"That's fine," he said, and closed his arms around her.

Chapter Four

Clint remembered another waitress a few years ago, in Abilene—one of the few pleasant memories of his time spent there—who reminded him of this one. The other woman had smelled the same—cooking smells—and her body tasted of salt and sweat, the way this one's did. That was just fine with Clint; he had a liking for girl-sweat and women smells.

Maggie was a mature woman with a full, firm body. She had large breasts, wide hips, well-rounded buttocks, and sleek, smooth skin.

Clint undressed her, lifted her up and carried her to the bed, enjoying the feel of her weight in his arms. The Gunsmith liked all kinds of women—the young ones, the slim ones included—but he always experienced a special kind of joy when he had his arms filled with a *lot* of woman.

She watched him from the bed as he undressed, and her eyes widened with delight when his swollen, pulsating penis came into view. Here was something she could really sink her teeth into—in a manner of speaking.

"I may be a waitress," she said with a smile, "but I'm through waiting."

She reached out and filled both of her hands with him, the right one taking hold of his swollen column, and the left palming his balls, and drew him to her that way. Her lips began to work on his belly, just above his pubic hair, while her hands continued to fondle him, and he brought both of his hands around to take hold of her head. She began to stroke his penis while her tongue flicked in and out of his navel, and then suddenly her head swooped down and she took a surprising amount of him into her hot and eager mouth. She began to suck avidly, working her mouth along the length of him, while her left hand continued to stroke and fondle his balls.

"Mmm," she murmured as she felt him swell even more, and she slid both hands behind him to dig her nails into his buttocks: At that moment a torrent of semen shot from him and cascaded down her throat, and she had no difficulty in accommodating all of it.

"Oh, yes," she said, releasing him from her mouth and pulling him down onto the bed next to her.

"My turn," he said. He rolled over and began to lick the sweaty salt from her breasts.

"I should have taken a bath before coming up," she said, "but I guess I was pretty eager."

"You don't need a bath," he said. "You're fine just the way you are."

"I'm sweaty."

"And delicious," he assured her. To illustrate his point he plunged his tongue into the deep valley between her breasts and proceeded to lick it clean. He then switched his attention to her pinkish nipples, sucking each of them to ultrahard points while she sighed and groaned in response. He moved his hand down and laid it on her round belly, and then used his fingers to poke into the golden patch of hair until he found her moist opening. He sank one finger into her to the knuckle, and then another, and she lifted her hips off the bed to meet the pressure of his hand.

"Oh, God," she said as he wiggled his fingers, and she began to squirm on the bed, as if trying to drive her bottom through the mattress. "Oh, do it," she said. "Please, do it."

She reached down and was pleasantly surprised to find that his cock was already hard again, and she grabbed it and said, "I want it, I want it now."

"Not yet," he said. He moved his hips, gently disengaging himself from her grasp, and then slid his fingers out of the warmth of her slippery tunnel. He moved down on the bed until his nose was being tickled by the downy growth between her legs and began to probe her fragrant pussy with his tongue, sliding up and down, and then in and out, being careful never to come in direct contact with her swollen button.

"Oh, God, Clint—" she started, but the words died in her mouth as he suddenly flicked his tongue upward without warning. Her hips began to jerk spasmodically and he used his forearms to pin her to the bed while he continued to circle her clit with his tongue. When her belly began to tremble he locked his lips around her inflamed bud and began to suck on it furiously.

"Oh, Jesus, don't stop, don't ever stop . . .," she said as she fought against the strength in his arms, trying to lift her ass off the bed. "Hold me down," she moaned. "Don't let me go . . . "

She was a big girl, and strong, but he didn't have much

difficulty in keeping her pinned while he worked on her, and then all of a sudden she erupted. He moved quickly, thrusting himself into her while she was still in the midst of her orgasm, and even before the first one ended, the second one began. She threw her legs around him as he drove in and out of her again and again, and then he tilted his head down so that he could suck one of her breasts while he fucked her.

"Oh, yes," she said, grasping the back of his head tightly while her legs and thighs tightened around his waist. "Never let you go," she said. "Never ever . . ."

He felt his own orgasm building up and knew that it was going to be something special, something that would hurt and feel incredibly good at the same time.

When it came he had to release her breast so that he could moan out loud. As his seed burst from him, pumping furiously, he felt the pain at the end of each spasm, but in between it was unbelievably good and in spite of the fact that it was his second time in less than fifteen minutes, it seemed as if it was never going to stop.

"Yes, yes . . ." she babbled as he continued to fill her up, stoking a fire inside of her that seemed totally unquenchable.

As he felt his spasms ending, he reached beneath her to grab the cheeks of her ample behind and hold her tightly to him, and as the last dregs of his seed were sucked out of him, everything seemed to fade out. . . .

Chapter Five

He awoke while she was getting dressed, and she smiled at him and said, "I've got to go back to work."

"How long—" he began.

"We slept for a couple of hours, which means I may be in trouble with my boss."

"I'll talk to him," he offered.

"You don't have to," she said. "I can handle him." She walked to the bed and leaned over it, adding, "Not the way I handled you, though."

"I should hope not."

She kissed him and as she straightened up there was a knock on the door.

"Your boss?" he asked.

"I doubt it," she said. "I came up the back way."

He stood up and pulled on his pants, then palmed his gun and said, "You want to go out the window or hide behind the door?"

She smiled and said, "Just open it."

He walked to the door holding his gun in his right hand, and used his left to open the door.

"Clint!" Bat Masterson said, with a big smile on his young face. He looked past the Gunsmith then, at Maggie, and a smile of another kind crossed his face. "Didn't waste any time, did you?"

"You weren't here," Clint replied with a shrug. "I had to do something to pass the time."

"I'll be going back to work now," Maggie said, stepping past the two men. "I'll see you again, Clint."

"Count on it," he said. He leaned out the door and both men watched her walk down the hall to the back stairway.

"That's a lot of woman," Bat said.

"I know," the Gunsmith answered. "You want to come in?"

"You want a drink?" Bat asked, bringing a bottle of whiskey out from behind his back.

"Come on in."

Clint stepped back into the room and put his gun back in the holster that was hanging on the bedpost. When he turned back to Bat the whiskey bottle was flying through the air towards him, and he reached out with his right hand and caught it.

"As quick as ever, I see," said Bat.

Clint shook his head and pulled the top off the bottle. He took a healthy swallow, then held it by the neck and passed it back to Bat.

"It's good to see you," he told the young man.

"You too," Bat said. He took a swallow of whiskey and passed the bottle back, then pulled a chair over and sat down. Clint sat on the bed and asked, "Now would you mind telling me why I'm here?"

"Right to the point, huh?" Bat asked. "What about what's happened between Willow Falls and now?"

"We can catch up after you tell me why I'm here," Clint said, then added, "If I'm still here, that is."

"What makes you think you wouldn't be?"

"As soon as I got to town and started looking for you the bartender in the saloon let me know that trouble was coming."

"Even if that's right," Bat said, "you wouldn't leave a friend in trouble, would you?"

Clint stared at Bat for a few seconds, then said, "If you thought I would, you wouldn't have sent for me, would you?"

"That's right."

Clint took another drink and then said, "Okay, then, let me have it. What kind of trouble is heading here, Bat?"

"We've heard there's quite a large number of Texans riding this way."

"So?" Clint asked. A quick flash of memory struck Clint, reminding him that it was a feud with Texans that had caused Abilene to explode the way it did, ending with the death of Texas saloon owner Phil Coe, and deputy Mike Williams. It had also been the beginning of the end for Wild Bill Hickok.

"The mayor is afraid that Bassett, Tilghman and I won't be able to control them. Bill Tilghman had a run-in with a tough name of Texas Bill and laid him and two of his friends out."

"Dead?"

Bat shook his head. "Bill only used his fists, and then marched the three of them off to jail. This happened a ways back, but the mayor and Bassett are afraid that these boys might be heading here to take the town apart."

"What kind of a lawman is Bassett?"

"Honest," Bat said. "Not flashy. He gets his job done."

"You figure you're going to need help?"

"I wouldn't have called for you if I didn't," Bat said.

"What about the mayor?"

"Our mayor is actually George Hoover, but a lot of people look to Dog Kelly, the owner of the Alhambra saloon, to make decisions. Kelly is supposed to be sending for some help of his own."

"Who?"

Bat shrugged and said, 'I guess we'll know that when they get here."

"I guess I could stick around that long," Clint said. "Depending on who comes in, you may not need me."

"Suit yourself," Bat said, "but there's no telling what kind of no-goods are going to respond to Kelly . . . if anyone responds at all."

"How do you get into these messes, Bat?"

"The same way you get into yours, Clint," he said. "I met Tilghman when I got here and we got along, and from there Bassett offered me the badge." Bat touched the star he was wearing on his chest. "I figured, why not? It's an experience."

"Yeah," Clint said. "So was Abilene."

"Speaking of Abilene," Bat said, "you'll be interested to know something about Bill Tilghman."

"What kind of a lawman is he?"

"He's a good man, Clint," Bat replied. "He's about my age, he does his job and he can handle a gun."

"How well?"

"Well enough," Bat said. "He learned from one of the best."

"Oh, who?"

"Hickok," Bat said, watching Clint for his reaction. "Bill learned how to shoot from Wild Bill Hickok."

Chapter Six

Bat Masterson's revelation made Clint want to meet Bill Tilghman. Hickok had been such a close friend of the Gunsmith's that he welcomed any kind of link with the dead legend.

"We'll try the Long Branch Saloon," Bat said as he and Clint left the hotel.

On the way to the Long Branch they passed several of Dodge City's other gambling establishments, like the Crystal Palace, the Junction Saloon, the Alamo—shades of Abilene!—the Lone Star, and others. Not a large town, Dodge had more than its share of gambling houses and saloons, and at times it appeared that the gamblers outnumbered the cowboys they victimized.

"I thought Dodge would be larger," Clint said as the two men walked down Front Street.

"There's enough trouble here for a town twice the size, believe me, Clint."

The Long Branch was probably the largest saloon and gambling hall in Dodge. If it wasn't, it was certainly the most prosperous.

When Clint and Bat entered the saloon, the Gunsmith saw what the bartender had meant about the town blossoming. The place was packed with cowboys, drinking, gambling and cavorting with the saloon girls.

"If he's in here we'll never find him," Clint said.

"Let's elbow our way to the bar and get a beer," Bat said. "If we don't find him in a while, we'll try the Lone Star."

"Are you sure this isn't just your way of getting me to do your rounds with you?"

Bat laughed and slapped his friend on the back. "Nice of you to offer. Come on."

Bat led the way to the bar, where he used both elbows to carve out a niche large enough for the two of them.

"Hey!" one man protested.

"Something on your mind, friend?" Bat asked, turning to face the man. Clint didn't know if the man recognized Bat, or simply saw the badge on his chest, but something mollified him.

"Uh, no, nothing," he said, and turned to face the other way.

"Two beers, Art," Bat told the bartender.

"Right away, Deputy."

"What's the story here, Bat?" Clint asked in a low voice. "You been throwing your weight around town or what?"

"Not me, Clint," Bat said, "but Tilghman's known to be pretty fast with his fists as well as his guns. When he flattened Texas Bill, he made some enemies, but he scared a lot of people too."

"So they stay out of his way, and yours?"

"I told you Bill and me have gotten pretty friendly."

"I can't wait to meet this guy," Clint said, picking up his beer.

At that moment a man came barreling through the batwing doors backwards, fell to the floor and tumbled end over end until he was stopped by the back of an occupied chair, almost upsetting it.

"What the—" the man in the chair yelled, turning around and looking down.

"Well, there he is now," Bat said.

"That's Tilghman?" Clint asked, looking at the man on the floor.

"No," Bat said, and when another man stepped through the batwing door, he added, "that's Tilghman."

Tilghman stood in the doorway looking around, and when he located the man on the floor he advanced on him.

"Get up, cowboy," he said.

"What's going on?" the man whose chair had been upset asked.

"Just sit tight, friend," Tilghman said as he hauled the other man to his feet. "This is between me and this fella, here."

The seated man stood up, towering over Tilghman, and said, "Yeah, well, that fella there happens to be my brother, friend."

"Oh, yeah?" Tilghman asked.

"Yeah," the man said, and then the other four men at the table stood up and he added, "and these are my friends."

"Oh, boy," Bat said, putting his beer down on the bar.

"He wouldn't," Clint said.

"Yes, he would," Bat answered, and as he did Tilghman swung and hit the big man, sending him down on his back on top of the table.

Both Clint and Bat moved away from the bar as the men at the table surged towards Tilghman.

"Move over, Bill," Bat said aloud. The sound of his voice attracted Tilghman's attention, just as somebody threw a punch at him. The force of the blow knocked Tilghman back a few steps, and Bat stepped into his place and returned the blow. Before long, a donnybrook was in full swing.

The two brothers and their friends were part of a trail drive and had come into town to wash away some trail dust. They also had one or two more friends in the saloon, who also joined in the fray.

None of the cowboys were wearing guns, so it didn't seem in order for Clint, Bat or Tilghman to draw theirs—none of the three of them would have shot an unarmed man—so the fight went on until Charlie Bassett stepped through the batwing doors and discharged a single barrel of a double-barrel shotgun into the ceiling.

"The fight's over, boys!" he shouted. He looked around and when his eyes found Tilghman—pinned to the floor by two cowboys—he said, "I might have known I'd find you in the middle of this."

"I was making a lawful arrest," Tilghman said in his own defense.

"I know," Bassett said. "That's always the case. Okay, get up from there."

The two cowboys got off of him so that the deputy could get up, and then Bassett said, "Okay, let's all take a walk to the jail."

The sheriff swung around and just happened to point his shotgun at Clint, but Bat stepped in and said, "Not him,

Charlie. He was just helping me and Bill out.''

"Yeah, sure," Bassett' said, eyeing the Gunsmith dubiously. Finally he relented and said, "Okay, he can stay and help Chalk and Bill clean up.''

Chalk Beeson and Bill Harris were the owners of the Long Branch Saloon, and Bill Harris had been standing on the side—where it was safe—tallying up the damages. He stepped forward now and gave the sheriff a piece of paper.

"Damages, Charlie," he said.

"Fine," Bassett said, taking it from him. "I'll see that you get paid."

"Hey, you ain't gonna make us pay for this, are you?" one of the brothers complained. "He started it," the man added, pointing at Tilghman.

"He always starts it," Bassett said, "but the damages will be added to your fine.''

"Fine? For what?"

"We'll talk about it at the jail," Bassett said, "with me on the outside and you on the inside. Then you can decide whether or not you want to pay.''

"Let's go," Tilghman said, giving the man a little shove from behind.

"Bill—" Bassett said shortly, and Tilghman raised both of his hands in front of him and shrugged.

"Stay here," Bat told Clint. "We'll be back in a little while.''

"Sure."

As the men filed out, with Bat bringing up the rear, Clint heard Harris call out to the bartender, "Okay, Art, let's get some tables out from the back and clean up this mess." To his customers he said, "Just be patient, folks, we'll have this place cleaned up in no time. One round of drinks on the house while you're waiting!''

As Harris started for the back Clint stepped in and said, "Mind if I give you a hand?"

The saloon owner stopped, looked at him and then said, "Why not? You helped break it up, so you might as well help put it back together again."

"My sentiments exactly," the Gunsmith said.

Chapter Seven

While a couple of the saloon girls cleaned up the debris, Clint helped the bartender and Bill Harris bring tables out of the back room, and about ten minutes after the fight had ended, things were back to normal in the Long Branch Saloon.

"Thanks for your help," Harris said while having a beer with Clint at the bar. "It usually takes a little longer and we lose a few customers."

"Glad to help."

"At least they didn't break the mirror or any glass this time," Harris went one.

"How often does this happen?"

Harris laughed. "Anytime Tilghman tries to make an arrest in here—or anywhere near here."

"I see. Fast with his hands, huh?"

"It's not that bad," Harris said. "He's fast with his gun too, but he'd rather use his hands. I guess that's good, huh?"

"I guess."

"I didn't catch your name, friend."

"Adams, Clint Adams," Clint answered, watching Harris closely. The name obviously registered with the man, as he would have expected it to. As the owner of a saloon like the Long Branch, Harris would have heard of most any man with a reputation, and the Gunsmith certainly had that.

"My God," Harris said, "the Gunsmith."

"Not so loud, okay?" Clint said. "When I hear that name it grates on my nerves."

"The way I hear it, you don't have any nerves," Harris said.

"Don't believe everything you hear."

"About you?"

"About anyone," Clint said. "Reputations are blown up all out of proportion."

"You don't like having a rep?" Harris asked.

"Does that surprise you?"

Harris thought a moment, then said, "I guess that depends on which rep we're talking about. I've heard that you were a hell of a lawman as well as being fast with a gun."

"I was a good lawman," Clint said simply.

"But not anymore?"

"Not anymore."

"Why are you here, then?" Harris asked.

"Bat and I are friends."

"Were you aware that trouble is coming?"

"Riding hard," Clint said. "I heard."

"I can't believe that Bassett won't try and pin a badge on you."

"He'll have a hard time pinning it to a moving target."

At that point both Bat and Bill Tilghman came walking in, laughing together.

"Oh, Christ, hide the breakables," Harris said as the two young men approached the bar.

"It wasn't my fault," Bill Tilghman said aloud, daring anyone to contradict him. Aside from being a little bigger and heavier than Bat, both men were quite alike in appearance—and very young. Clint couldn't remember when he was that young.

"Two beers, Art," Bat called out. He looked around and said, "You sure got the place cleaned up in record time."

"We've had a lot of practice," Harris said, looking pointedly at Tilghman. "Besides, your friend helped."

"My friend," Bat said, as if reminding himself that Clint was there. "Clint, this is Bill Tilghman. Bill, Clint Adams."

"I've been looking forward to meeting you," Tilghman said, extending his hand. "I've heard a lot about you."

"I've been hearing a lot about you since I got to town," Clint replied.

"I can imagine," Tilghman said, picking up his beer.

"I hear you learned how to shoot from Bill Hickok."

"Yeah, old Jim," Tilghman said, smiling at some fond memory. Many of Hickok's friends called him by his proper name—"Jim" for James Butler Hickok—but Clint had never gotten into that habit. His friend was always "Bill" to him. "That was so long ago."

"Oh? How long?"

"God, I was twelve years old," Tilghman said, surprising Clint. "He came riding by our farm and I was out shooting targets and not hitting anything. He got off his horse and started showing me how it was done. He stayed around and gave me a few lessons, showing me how to draw. 'All in the wrist,' he'd say."

"Twelve years old," Clint repeated. "From what I hear you've learned your lessons very well."

"Don't believe everything you hear," Bill Harris chimed in.

"Hey, what's that mean?" Tilghman asked, good naturedly.

"Just repeating something somebody told me once," Harris said. "I've got to go take care of some business, boys. Drink up."

"Charlie's got your money, Bill," Bat said. "You can pick it up whenever you're ready."

"Hey," Harris said, "that's the business I was talking about. See you later."

After Harris left Clint said, "He seems to take getting his place busted up in stride."

"Any saloon owner has to expect that," Tilghman said.

"Especially when you're around, right?" Bat asked.

"Don't blame me," Tilghman said. "You were in there throwing punches, too."

"What did you arrest that guy for, anyway?" Clint asked.

"I wasn't gonna arrest him," Tilghman said. "Not until he threw a punch at me."

"What'd you say to him to make him do that?" Bat asked.

"Look, it was just a misunderstanding," Tilghman said. "The guy's from Texas, so he can't be right in the head, anyway."

Clint didn't want to touch that line and Bat said, "Texas—that reminds me."

"Are you gonna start that again?" Tilghman asked. "I

told you we can handle anything that comes along.''

"What about the help Dog Kelly is getting us?''

"Knowing Dog Kelly, I can just imagine what kind of help he's getting us. No, I think we're gonna have to do this on our own . . . unless your friend here—'' Tilghman stopped as if he'd just realized something and looked straight at Bat Masterson. "You sent for him, didn't you?''

"Well, yeah,'' Bat admitted. "I figured he could protect us from the people Dog Kelly was bringing in to help us.''

Tilghman seemed about to say one thing, then changed his mind and said, "You know, that ain't a half bad idea.''

Chapter Eight

When Clint offered to buy dinner at his hotel, Bat accepted, but Tilghman begged off.

"I'll see you boys tomorrow," he said, and left the Long Branch without saying where he was going.

"I think he's got someone hidden away somewhere," Bat said.

"That's his business."

Bat gave Clint an odd look and said, "Sure, I guess. When do you want to eat?"

"Let's go now," Clint said.

"Lead the way."

When they got to the hotel dining room Clint was only peripherally aware of the fact that Maggie Lane was not there. He had something else on his mind, and Bat recognized that fact.

"Look," he said after they had ordered dinner, "nobody is going to try to force you to pin on a badge, you know."

''How did you know I was thinking about that?''

Bat shrugged and said, ''There's some kind of a burr under your saddle. I took a shot.''

''Your shot was right on the money, as usual.''

''Coming from you, I'll take that as a great compliment,'' Bat replied. ''Look, Bassett doesn't have to know anything more than that we're friends. If trouble starts while you're here, though, I don't think he'd mind if you chipped in.''

''I don't think he was too happy with my contribution to the fight in the Long Branch.''

''Don't worry, I told him about that. You couldn't just stand there and watch me get pounded into the floor, could you?'' When Clint didn't answer right away Bat said, ''Don't be so quick to answer, pal.''

''I had to think about it,'' Clint explained.

''Thanks a lot.''

Dinner came and they finally settled down and caught up on what had happened since they had last met. Bat was especially interested in Clint's frank explanation of how he had reacted to the shooting death of Wild Bill Hickok, and thought that he himself would probably have reacted that way to the death of Wyatt Earp, or even the Gunsmith, if they had been killed in the same manner. Bat held both Earp—who was only four or five years older— and Clint Adams in a special kind of awe, though he wouldn't openly admit it to anyone.

''I think I can understand why you reacted the way you did,'' he told Clint.

''Really?'' Clint asked. ''It took me a while to understand it myself, but when I did I straightened up.''

''Glad to hear that.''

''What about you?'' Clint asked, wanting to get off the subject of himself.

Bat explained that he had traveled a lot, crossed paths with Wyatt Earp a couple of times, gambled mostly, while trying to stay out of trouble.

"Gambling and trouble go hand in hand," Clint said, "and for that matter, so do you and trouble."

"That's cruel," Bat said, "but fairly accurate. Then again, the same can be said of you."

"Unfortunately."

"Face it, Clint. When a man can handle a gun the way you do—I don't think you could go back and do it all over again differently."

"Maybe I couldn't," Clint said, "but I'd welcome the chance to try."

After dinner they went back to the Long Branch to gamble. Disdaining faro, roulette and some of the other house games, they found two empty chairs at a back-table poker game between some townspeople and proceeded to clean up, virtually splitting the profits between them.

Having had his afternoon nap interrupted—although pleasantly so—Clint quit the game before Bat did, bidding his friend good night. Bat was glad to see the Gunsmith leave, because it meant that from that point on he'd be the only winner at the table. Clint recognized this from the look on the younger man's face and was laughing to himself as he walked back along Front Street to his hotel.

As he approached the front of the hotel he heard someone call out to him from a darkened doorway, and turned to find Maggie beckoning to him.

"What are you doing hiding in doorways?" he asked her, stepping in with her.

"I don't want my boss to see me," she said. "He gave me hell for coming back late this afternoon."

"I'm sorry."

"Don't be," she said, dropping her hand to his crotch.

"It was worth it."

"But what are you doing hiding out here?"

"Waiting for you," she said. "I'm being bold again, but if you want me tonight, I don't want to be seen going up to your room. I thought I would take you to my room."

"Maggie, I'd like to—" he began.

"My bed is much more comfortable than the one in your hotel room," she said. "I can promise you that."

"I have to get some sleep," he warned her.

"So do I," she said. "Nobody says we have to make love all night—although it might be interesting to try."

"Not tonight, it wouldn't," he said. "All right, woman, you talked me into it. Lead the way."

Eagerly she grabbed his hand and began to pull him along. She cut through an alley and brought him out onto Bridge Street, where she lived in a room above and behind the general store. They had to ascend a stairway on the side of the building, and she released his hand long enough to get her key out and open the door, then grabbed it again and pulled him in.

"Shall I light a lamp?" she asked.

He pulled on her hand now, spinning her into his embrace, and kissed her long and hard.

"I don't think we need any light to find each other," he asked her. "Do you?"

She touched his crotch again and felt his penis hard and ready, and said, "No, sir!"

Chapter Nine

Clint woke briefly the next morning as Maggie slipped from the bed, explaining that she had to be at work early to serve breakfast. He watched with pleasure as she padded about the room naked, then as she dressed, and when she had kissed him and left, he dozed off again, to awaken a mere half an hour later. He went back to the hotel for a fresh change of clothes, then used the hotel bath facilities. Feeling refreshed and wide awake, he went to the dining room for breakfast, and was waited on by Maggie, who saw to it that he got a little extra of everything in his plate. While he was enjoying his breakfast, both Bat Masterson and Bill Tilghman entered, and he waved them over.

"Hey," Bat said, noticing the amount of food he had in his plate, "you must know someone in the kitchen, huh?"

"I've got friends all over, Bat," Clint said. "You should know that. I'm a very friendly guy."

"Especially when your friends look like that, huh?"

Bat said, inclining his head in Maggie's direction.

Tilghman looked over at Maggie, then said, "Nice, but a little old for me."

"You'll find as you get older, Bill," Clint said, sounding like an old philosopher, "that women *don't* get older, they just get more experienced."

"And an experienced woman can be a revelation," Bat finished.

Tilghman gave Bat a funny look and Bat said, "I've heard this speech before."

Clint called Maggie over and she took both of the other men's orders for breakfast, then asked Clint if he needed anything else. He told her he was fine.

"Well, one thing's for sure," Bat said as she left. "You'll be well fed while you're in Dodge."

All three were eating breakfast when a young boy came in, searched the room, and then approached their table, carrying a telegram.

"For you, Deputy," he said, handing it to Tilghman, who took it and flipped the boy a coin.

"Bad news," Bat said.

"How can you tell?" Clint asked.

"Just a feeling," Bat answered as he watched Tilghman tear it open and read it. "Well, what's it say?"

"Clay Allison."

"It's from Clay Allison?" Clint asked, surprised.

"No," Tilghman said, shaking his head. 'It's about Clay Allison."

"What about him?"

"He's on his way here."

"With this big group of Texans that are supposed to be on the way?"

"He's not part of that crowd," Tilghman said, folding

the telegram. "This is something else, something personal."

Clint looked to Bat for more of an explanation. "When Allison heard what Bill did to Texas Bill, he started bragging that he would gun Tilghman down before he could ever get close enough to use his fists." Bat turned to Tilghman and asked, "How long before he gets here?"

"A day or two, I guess, depending on how hard he rides," Tilghman answered. "Telegram was sent by a friend of mine in Oklahoma. Allison was bragging that he was on his way here to take care of me." He shoved the envelope into his pocket and said, "Come on, let's finish eating."

"Are you going to show that telegram to Charlie?" Bat asked.

"What for?"

"He's the sheriff; he should know if trouble is heading into Ford County."

"You mean more trouble?"

"That's right, more trouble, only this ain't his trouble or the town's trouble, it's mine. I'll take care of it myself."

"Bassett is the sheriff, like Bat said," Clint remarked after listening to them for a few minutes. "You better tell him that Clay Allison is coming to his town."

Tilghman looked at Bat, who shrugged and said, "The voice of experience."

Tilghman alternated his glance between the two of them a few times, then shrugged and said, "Okay, so I'll tell Charlie about it. It's still my problem."

"Clay Allison is a handful, the way I hear it," Clint said.

"Yeah, well, ask around," Tilghman said, standing

up. "See what people say about me."

"Where are you going?" Bat asked him. "You didn't finish your breakfast."

"You want me to talk to Bassett, I'm going to talk to Bassett," Tilghman said. "Pay my bill, will you?"

"Sure," Bat said. "Sure."

They both watched Tilghman's retreating back until he left the room, and then Bat said, "He's a little touchy sometimes."

"If I had somebody like Clay Allison coming to town to blow my head off I'd be touchy, too."

"I doubt it," Bat said. "Not you, and not Bill, either. He's not worried about Allison. He just gets touchy sometimes. You could have told him to pass the salt, and if he didn't feel like it, he'd get touchy."

"So you don't think he's worried about Clay Allison?"

"Not at all. Bill knows he can take Allison."

"Is that so?"

"Sure. He also knows he could take me or you or that he could have taken Bill Hickok, if he wanted to."

Clint took a few moments to finish the scraps of food that were left in his plate, and then to pour himself another cup of coffee. That done he looked at Bat, who had not taken his eyes off the Gunsmith during the entire three minute ritual, and said, "Bill Tilghman has a definite attitude problem, Bat."

"Nah," Bat said, shaking his head. "He's just confident, that's all."

"Wrong," Clint said. "He's cocky. That's not being confident, that's an invitation to getting killed."

Chapter Ten

That afternoon Bassett asked Clint to join him in his office, and then offered him a badge.

"No."

"Why not?"

"I don't wear a badge anymore, Sheriff."

"You got something against the law?"

"No," Clint answered. "It's a personal thing."

"Do you know what kind of trouble is heading for this town?" the lawman asked.

"I've got a good idea, yeah."

"We're gonna need all the help we can get, Adáms," Bassett said.

"Against the Texans, or Clay Allison?"

"Clay Allison?" Bassett asked, looking puzzled. "Who said anything about Clay Allison?"

"Oh," Clint said. "Uh—"

"Is Clay Allison, the killer, coming to Dodge?"

"That's what I heard," Clint said slowly.

"Jesus Christ. What's he want here?"

"Apparently he and Tilghman have a date with destiny."

"A what?"

"They're going to face off."

"You mean Allison isn't coming in with the Texans?"

"No. He and Tilghman have something personal going. Your deputy was going to tell you about it a little later in the day, so if I was you, I wouldn't even mention that I said anything."

"Uh-huh," Bassett said. He was staring off into space, contemplating the consequences of Clay Allison's visit to Dodge. "After all," he said, "He's just another killer. We've had our share of them here. I mean, look at you—" Suddenly he stopped short, as if realizing what he was saying. "I mean—I didn't mean to say—uh—"

"Forget it, Sheriff," Clint said. "Look, I'll be around town for a while, so if there's any trouble and I can help, I will—but I won't pin on a badge. Fair enough?"

"Uh, sure, that's fair," Bassett said. "I appreciate that, Adams, I really do."

"No problem. I'll stay in touch."

"Thanks, Adams."

Clint nodded and left the sheriff safe in the knowledge that he had commissioned one "killer" to take care of another.

Chapter Eleven

Clint's next stop was where he had been headed when Bassett intercepted him—the bank. He had left Texas in such a hurry to answer Bat's summons that he hadn't taken very much cash with him, so he decided to go to the Dodge City Bank and have them wire his bank to enable him to withdraw some cash to hold him until he got back to Texas to pick up his rig—or until he hit it big in a poker game.

When he approached the teller in the first of three windows he was referred to Miss Vining at a desk to his right. When he turned to approach her, Miss Vining was standing, making an attempt to adjust the swivel chair behind her desk. Clint pulled himself up short and just stood there, watching the young lady wrestle with the chair.

Amy Vining was the object of many of the young men's—and half the older ones'—fantasies in Dodge, and had been for the past three years, since she left the farm to live and work in town. At nineteen she had blossomed into a lovely, if somewhat . . . meaty young woman. Blond, with a wide, full-lipped mouth, Amy had full, well-rounded breasts and broad hips. She was one of those women who really *was* pleasingly plump. Her wide, blue eyes reflected an innocence that most men found challenging, while her full body simply aroused the baser of men's instincts.

Just seeing her bent over her chair, with her back to him, was arousing Clint's interest right on the spot. When she had apparently adjusted the chair to her liking she turned and caught the Gunsmith watching her. She held his eyes boldly for a moment, then allowed them to slide away as she sat down.

Clint covered the space between him and Miss Vining's desk and said, "Excuse me?"

Bright blue eyes looked up at him inquiringly and she asked, "Can I help you?"

"Yes, I believe you can," he said.

"Why don't you sit down, sir, and tell me how?"

Clint pulled a chair over, sat down, stared into this disturbingly appealing girl's blue eyes and told her what his problem was.

"There's no problem there, Mr. Adams," she said, sliding a pad and pencil over to his side of the desk. "If you'll just give me the name and location of your bank, I think I can get you a bank draft in no time."

"That's very efficient of you, Miss Vining," he said.

"Not at all."

He wrote down the pertinent information and passed the pad back to her.

"Why don't you check back with me later today, just

before closing time," she suggested. "I should have something for you by then."

Since he already had a legitimate excuse to come back and see her later in the day, he decided not to proffer any sort of invitation right there and then. He felt that this young woman had to be handled very carefully, and he didn't want to do anything to make her think that he was thinking the thoughts that he was thinking. Not just yet, anyway. He had found that women enjoy having men think about them that way, if they found out about it under the correct circumstances.

"Very well, Miss Vining," he said, standing up. "I'll see you later this afternoon, then."

He thought he saw something pass over her face just then, a puzzled or disappointed look, and then she said, "I'll look forward to it, Mr. Adams. Have a good day."

"Same to you," he said and, as much as he would have liked to back out of the bank, he turned his back to her and walked straight out without looking back.

Amy Vining sat at her desk, staring at the doorway for a few moments after Clint Adams had left. She knew very well what kind of thoughts had been going on inside that man's head, and wondered why he had not made some kind of an overture to her. Other men in town were always making remarks or extending shrouded—and some not so shrouded—invitations to her and she always knew how to handle them, because none of them interested her. This man, however, was different. For some reason when she had turned around to find him staring at her, something had fluttered in her stomach. She couldn't understand why this particular man had affected her that way, or why he had not said anything to her outside of the business they were transacting.

It was the first time she had ever wanted a man to approach her, and he hadn't done it.

Then again, he *was* coming back later, wasn't he?

Chapter Twelve

Clint found Bat Masterson making his afternoon rounds and walked along with him, telling him about his visit to the sheriff.

"Charlie's been known to step on his tongue from time to time, Clint," Bat said in response to Bassett's crack about killers. "Don't take it personal."

"I didn't take it personal, don't worry. I've dealt with people like Bassett before."

"Charlie's not that bad—" Bat started to defend his boss.

"No, I know that, he's just a little ignorant. I can overlook that . . . for a time."

They walked together for a block or so and then Bat said, "You got something else on your mind?"

"Yes, I do. I just came from the bank."

"You need a loan?"

"No, I don't need a loan. Any money I get from you I can take over a poker table."

"What a dreamer," Bat said, looking at the sky.

"I talked to a young lady at the bank and she's going to see about transferring some funds for me."

"A young lady? Blond, with big—"

"That's the one. Miss Vining."

Bat was nodding vigorously. "Amy Vining. Clint, my friend, you have no idea how many men in this town have their eye on the delicious Miss Vining."

"Present company included?"

"Oh, I made my try. I think the young lady likes older men."

"What about Tilghman?"

"He ain't older."

"I mean has he made his play yet?"

"I don't think he has any interest in her. He likes skinny girls. Why all the questions?"

"I just don't want to graze on another man's range."

"Well, you ain't on mine or Bill's, so good luck, but I have to warn you. She may make your blood boil, but she's been a cold fish as long as I been in this town."

"Well, I got one thing in my favor right off," Clint said.

"Oh? What's that?"

"If she likes older men, she can't get one much older than me. I feel about a hundred."

"I guess that comes from carrying around a heavy, unwanted rep, huh, pal?"

Clint grinned at his young friend and said, "I guess so. You're making a little reputation for yourself too, aren't you?"

"How do you mean?"

"I've heard about you from time to time, Bat. You got into a couple of scrapes with Wyatt—who's got a nice rep of his own. You, Wyatt, me—we attract trouble like honey draws flies, don't we?"

"I guess so," Bat said. "I only hope that me and Wyatt can make it to your age, old-timer, and look back with better memories and not nearly so much bitterness."

"Bitterness," Clint repeated. "Yeah, I guess I come off pretty bitter at times, don't I, Bat?"

"You don't have to, Clint," Bat said. "I've got a hell of a lot of respect for you. So does Wyatt, and so do a lot of other people. You don't earn respect like that without doing something right."

Clint stopped walking and looked at young Bat Masterson, who took another step or two and then stopped and turned to face the Gunsmith.

"You're pretty smart for a kid, aren't you?"

Bat grinned and said, "I hang around with the right people."

"Yeah," Clint said, putting his right hand on the younger man's shoulder and giving it an affectionate squeeze, "So do I."

Chapter Thirteen

Clint left Bat to the remainder of his rounds and went over to the Long Branch for a drink and, if he could find it that early, a game of poker.

"Hello, there," Bill Harris greeted him as he came in.

"Mr. Harris."

"Oh, call me Bill, everyone in town does. What can we get for you today?"

"A beer would be good, to start."

Harris turned to the bartender and said, "Art, get the man a beer, on the house."

"That's neighborly of you, Bill," Clint said. He looked around the room, which was empty except for a couple of guys drinking at different tables, a house dealer who was fiddling with a deck of cards, and a saloon girl who looked pretty bored.

"Here's your beer," Harris said, calling Clint's attention to the overflowing mug.

"Thanks."

"This place'll pick up in an hour or so, then just keep building until the walls start to give."

"That's the way to run a business," Clint said, sipping his beer.

"Hey, here comes my partner," Harris said, looking past Clint. He leaned closer and said, "Do you mind if I mention about, uh, you being the Gunsmith, and all?"

Clint figured he owed him something for helping bust up his place the night before, and the free beer, so he said, "You can mention the name, but I don't know about the 'all.' "

"Thanks."

Clint turned and saw a tall, slim man in his forties approaching. Harris was shorter, probably about five eight, and a few years younger.

"Chalk, I want you to meet somebody."

"Sure," the taller man said. He came up and stood next to Harris, facing Clint.

"Clint, I want you to meet my partner, Chalk Beeson. Chalk, this here's Clint Adams, otherwise known as—"

"The Gunsmith!" Beeson said, sounding and looking impressed. "It's a pleasure to meet you, Mr. Adams."

"Just Clint, please," Clint said, shaking the man's hand.

"I've heard a lot about you, Clint."

"Don't believe everything you hear," Harris said, giving Clint a conspiratorial look.

"I believe what I see," Beeson said. He turned to Clint and said, "I saw you in action once, years ago, in Oklahoma."

"Is that a fact?"

"Sure is. I ain't never seen nothing like it before or since. Why, I'd bet on you against anybody, even Bill Hickok himself."

"Bill was a friend of mine," Clint said, unable to keep the coldness out of his voice.

Although Chalk Beeson did not physically move, his partner sensed the man taking a mental step backward.

"I—I'm sorry," Beeson stammered. "I didn't mean anything."

"Forget it," Clint said. "It was nice meeting you, Mr. Beeson. You have a nice place here."

Clint held Beeson's eyes for a moment, and then the man said, "Yes, well, I have some, uh, paperwork to take care of. Billy, I'll, uh, I'll see you later."

"Sure, Chalk."

Beeson gave the Gunsmith one last unsteady look, and then turned and walked to the back office. In fact, if Beeson had not turned and left at that moment, Clint would have.

"I'm sorry about that," Bill Harris said. "Chalk, he's got this fascination with men who have reputations."

"Don't you?"

"Sure, but not like Chalk. He's like a little kid when it comes to—well, you know—"

"Killers?"

"Legends," Harris said. "Especially living legends."

Living legends, the Gunsmith thought, shaking his head. Wild Bill Hickok was the only man he had ever known who might have fit that description. He certainly never thought of himself that way. Then again, he rarely thought of himself as anything but Clint Adams, the kid from the East who had come West to find—what? What had he come West to find? It was so many years ago that he'd forgotten. He only knew that he hadn't been looking for what he'd ultimately found.

He swirled the remainder of the beer in his mug, watching it go round and round, then finished it off and slapped the empty mug down on the bar.

"Thanks for the beer," he said.

"Have another."

"One'll do. Maybe later I'll come back for the other one."

"Try some of our games, Clint," Harris invited. "Our dealers are the best in town."

"Maybe I'll do that too," he said.

Then again, he thought as he walked out, maybe he'd start doing his drinking at one of the other saloons in town.

Chapter Fourteen

Amy Vining was annoyed to find herself watching the clock and the front door, waiting for the reappearance of the man called Clint Adams. Clint didn't know it, but this was why she was so surprised when she looked up from her desk and suddenly found him standing there.

"Oh!" she said. "You startled me!"

"I'm sorry," he said. He was busy admiring her eyes, which had widened so much at the sight of him. "I didn't mean to."

"That's all right. Why don't you sit down, Mr. Adams? I've taken care of everything for you."

"You have?"

"I told you it wouldn't be hard."

"Nothing's hard when you put your mind to it," he replied. "For instance, I'll bet that I could get you to go to dinner with me this evening, if I tried hard enough."

"Really?" she asked. Now the man had surprised her by getting personal right away. She had the feeling that he was trying to cause her to lose her balance, and decided to push back, a little. Her father had always told her, ''Push back, or get pushed over.'' It seemed to apply here. ''Of course, that would be assuming that I didn't want to go with you in the first place.''

She enjoyed the confused look on his face as he said, ''Uh, well, that's right.''

She scribbled on a small slip of paper, signed her name, then handed it to him and said, ''I think you'll find that's the figure we discussed.''

He took it from her and looked at it. ''That's the amount, all right.''

''Take it to the teller and he'll give you the cash, Mr. Adams,'' she instructed.

''That's fine,'' he said, ''but once I have the cash, I'm going to need something to spend it on.''

''I'm afraid I can't help you with that,'' she said, ''unless you want to invest it.''

''That sounds like a good idea,'' he said. ''Would you like to help me invest it in a couple of steak dinners tonight?''

''Is this your idea of trying hard enough?'' she asked him.

''No,'' he said. ''I'm just asking you to have dinner with me, Miss Vining.''

She lowered her eyes for a moment, then looked at him and said, ''My name is Amy, and I'd be pleased to have dinner with you . . . Clint.''

''Good,'' he said. ''What time do you finish here?''

''In about fifteen minutes, but I'll have to go home and change,'' she said.

''Where do you live?''

She smiled and said, ''I've got a room right upstairs. It

sort of came with the job. You see, my father used to be a farmer, but now he's the manager of the bank.''

"That's a neat trick," he said. "Why don't you tell me about it over dinner."

She smiled and said, "Okay. Will you come by for me at seven?"

"Sure," he said, standing up. "I better get my money before the window closes, or we'll be eating beef jerky and beans. See you in a little while."

"Okay, Clint."

She watched him as he went to the window to get his money, and then gave him a little wave before he walked out the door. She looked at the clock then. In fifteen minutes she'd be upstairs in the bath, soaping herself thoroughly, washing her hair, getting herself fixed up like she hadn't done in a long, long time, and all for a man she'd just met that afternoon.

Push back or get pushed over. She got a funny feeling in the pit of her stomach as she realized that where Clint Adams was concerned, she might not mind getting pushed over.

As she had planned, Amy was in the bath fifteen minutes later. She rubbed the soap vigorously between her hands, creating mountains of lather, and then began to rub her hands over her full breasts, thinking about Clint Adams as she did so. Her nipples got hard as she continued to soap herself, and that funny feeling that had been in the pit of her stomach earlier moved down even lower.

Closing her eyes she placed the palm of her hand between her legs and began to move it up and down, still thinking about Clint Adams.

Amy wasn't a virgin—not since almost a year before,

when she had given in to a boy she had grown up with, just to see what it was like. She hadn't been terribly impressed at the time, but she had the feeling that it might be different with a man like Clint.

Letting her head loll back against the lip of the tub, she increased the pressure of her hand between her legs and wondered idly if Clint thought she was a virgin.

Would he be disappointed to find out that she wasn't?

While Clint Adams was picking up Amy Vining for dinner—and whatever else the two of them decided they wanted to happen between them—Clay Allison was camped on a rise just outside of Dodge City. Allison had no intention of riding in at night. He knew that's what Tilghman would be expecting, but the dark would work in the deputy's favor, not his. Dodge was Tilghman's town and he knew his way around.

Clay Allison poured himself another cup of coffee to go with his beans. He'd ride in come morning, when the daylight worked for both of them. Tilghman was a fast man with his fists, they said, but Allison would never let him get that close. He'd gun him down in front of the whole town, and add Tilghman's name to his rep. Then maybe he could go another couple of months without some young kid trying to take him and make a name for himself.

Allison was thirty-six years old, and the way he figured to make it until he was thirty-seven was to keep people afraid of him. When people were afraid of you, they left you alone and they stayed out of your way. It was when they stopped hearing your name and stopped being afraid of you that somebody figured that maybe you were ripe to be taken.

Clay Allison vowed never to become that ripe.

Deputy Bill Tilghman's rounds took him to the very northern edge of town, and when he looked up at the rise there he saw the flicker of the campfire.

He knew it was Clay Allison.

Allison wasn't dumb. He'd wait until daylight before he rode into town, and when he did, Tilghman would make himself easy to find. He wasn't afraid of Allison, or of anyone else. He imagined himself—perhaps rightly so—the equal, or better, of any man with a gun. He had seen Bat handle a gun, and figured they were at least equals. He had never seen Hickok or the Gunsmith in action, but at times Bat seemed in awe of Adams—and Wyatt Earp, for that matter, although in Earp's case it wasn't necessarily because of his ability with a gun.

Although Tilghman admittedly had not gotten on very well with Adams since they met, he didn't mind having the man around. His gun probably would come in handy when that group of Texans finally rode into town. Allison, however, was another matter entirely. That was personal, and Tilghman would handle it himself. He knew that Adams had told Bassett about it—and Charlie had run up and down Tilghman's back about it—but Tilghman knew that Charlie wouldn't interfere, as long as it was simply Tilghman facing Allison.

Tilghman didn't know exactly what it was that made Allison so all fired eager to face him, but he intended to make the man regret the day he'd made that decision—if not the very day he had been born.

Chapter Fifteen

Contrary to Amy Vining's fears, it did not matter at all to Clint Adams that she was not a virgin. In truth, he had not expected her to be. Not with a face and a body like that.

The evening had started out innocently enough, with conversation over dinner. Actually, it started prior to that, with the decision of where to have dinner.

"The Dodge House has an excellent dining room," she told him when he picked her up.

Yes, he thought, *but they also have a waitress named Maggie*. He did not want to have to deal with a jealous female this evening, especially if she should be serving hot soup.

"I've eaten there every meal since I arrived in town," he said. "Do you know of somewhere else? Isn't there a nice little café?"

It was his experience that in every town, tucked out of the way, there was always a "nice little café" where the food was as good as home cooking. Dodge should be no exception.

"Well, yes, there is," she said, "but it's not on the main street."

"Good," he said. "That means the food will be worth what we pay for it."

"We?" she asked, teasingly.

"Just a slip of the tongue, Amy. Of course, dinner is on me. Lead the way."

The café was very much like the others Clint had been in, except that in this case the food was terrible.

"I'm sorry," Amy said at one point during the meal, "but I didn't remember it as being this bad."

"Don't worry," he said. "Being here with you more than makes up for the food."

"Thank you."

She talked about how her father had only bought their farm because of her mother, and never had much luck in trying to make something of it. It was after her mother died that she and her father moved into town and he became the bank manager, an occupation he was much more suited for. She began working in the bank as a teller, and had been steadily rising in her position.

"Maybe one day *I'll* be the bank manager," she finished.

"I'll bet you'd be a great bank manager," Clint said.

"I know I would be."

"Here's to Miss Amy Vining," Clint said, raising his coffee cup, "bank manager."

"I'll drink to that," she said, raising her own cup and clinking it against his.

"Are we finished here?" he asked.

She looked down at the empty plates and said, "I think so. Why?"

"I want to do something else."

"Like what?"

He put his coffee cup down and leaned his elbows on the table. "Do you live with your father?"

"Yes, I do."

"Would you like to go back to my room with me?"

She stared at him for a moment with those bright, clear blue eyes, then said, "Yes, Clint, I would, very much."

He touched her hand and said, "Let's go, then."

He held her hand as they left the café, and he could feel that she was trembling. She could have been frightened, but if she was feeling what he was feeling, she was trembling from eagerness.

As they approached the hotel she put her hand on his arm and he thought for a moment that she was going to change her mind, but she simply said, "I don't think I should be seen going in the front."

"I'll go to the back and open the door for you," he said. "Be there waiting for me, okay?"

"I won't change my mind, Clint," she said. "Don't worry."

Clint went into the hotel, through the lobby to the hall that led to the back door, and opened it, half expecting not to find Amy there.

She was standing there with her hands clasped in front of her, and when he opened the door she smiled and said, "Here I am."

"Nervous?" he asked her.

"Yes . . . and excited."

"Come on," he said, drawing her inside and shutting the door. She preceded him up the steps and when he unlocked the door to his room he allowed her to enter ahead of him.

He turned up the lamp, and then turned to face her. She

was standing as she had been at the back door, with her hands clasped in front of her, and he asked her again, "Nervous?"

She grinned and said, "Yes. But I'm not a virgin, you know." She blurted it out in a hurry, as if anxious to assure him of that fact.

"That doesn't matter," he said.

"I just wanted you to know."

"All right," he said, walking up to her and putting his hands on her shoulders. "Now I know."

Clint pulled her to him and kissed her. Her wide, full-lipped mouth opened eagerly beneath his, and their tongues fenced and intertwined as the kiss deepened. It went on and on, as if it would never end, and he became conscious of the intense heat that was emanating from her body, right through her clothing. He wanted to feel that heat up close, with nothing between them to block it off.

He reached behind her and began to undo the buttons on her simple, high-necked dress, then peeled it forward over her round shoulders, and down. She wiggled about some, which caused the dress to fall to the floor, and then she kicked it away. A few more deft movements of his practiced fingers, and her breasts blossomed against his chest, flattening themselves out as her distended nipples poked at him.

"You," she murmured against his mouth. "Now you."

Their mouths fused together again as both of them worked on his clothes, until they had to drift apart in order to finish undressing.

"I'll turn down the bed," she said, and he watched her with pleasure as she did so. She bent over, presenting him with a tantalizing view of her rounded buttocks, and as she pulled down the covers on the bed her full breasts dangled and swayed, and even slapped together lightly once or twice.

He approached her from behind, and as she was bent over he allowed his erect penis to slide along the cleft between her buttocks. She caught her breath as she felt the heat and smoothness of him, and the size, and when she turned she gathered his manhood into her hands and rubbed the swollen tips of her breasts against him. He cupped her face in his hands and kissed her again, and they tumbled to the bed that way, with nothing between them now to cut down on the heat they felt from each other.

He slid his mouth away from her and began to kiss her neck, and her shoulders. Slowly he worked his way down to her breasts, then ran his tongue between them, along the swollen undersides, and finally over the erect studs of her pink nipples.

"Oh, Clint," she moaned as he began to bite and suck her nipples, at the same time squeezing her breasts with his hands. "Oh, yes," she said, sliding her arms around him, running the flat palms of her hands over his back. "Oh, Lord, yes, Clint."

He slid his right hand down her body, over her belly and then ran his fingers along the lips of her second mouth, the vertical one which lay nestled between her legs like a precious jewel. When he spread the moist lips and dipped his finger into her, her breath caught again and she groaned aloud, raising her hips. He was struck then by the similarities between Amy and Maggie, and realized that the waitress was probably what Amy would look like in eighteen years or so.

"Please," she whispered hoarsely. "Now, don't make me wait."

"I want it to last," he said.

"Later," she said, "later it can last. Please . . ."

"All right," he said. He kissed her nipples, and then her mouth, and then he mounted her and slowly slid the length of his penis into her while she bit her bottom lip and moaned deep in her throat.

"Oh, God, I can't believe it . . ." she said as he slowly withdrew and then eased into her again.

"Believe it," he told her, "and enjoy it."

"I am." She smiled mischievously and said, "But I have a feeling I would enjoy it more if you would stop treating me as if I was breakable."

"Oh, really?"

"Yes, really," she said. She picked up her head and ran her tongue along his lips, and then he took it in his mouth as he worked his hands beneath her to cup her buttocks.

He withdrew from her slowly, inch by inch and then, without warning, slammed into her forcefully. If his mouth had not been on hers she would have screamed aloud, but her scream was muffled and ended in a long, drawn out moan.

He took hold of her buttocks tightly and began taking her in long, hard strokes, and she wrapped her plump thighs around his waist and braced her heels against the backs of his thighs.

"Yes, oh, yes," she murmured as he drove into her. "Do it, Clint, keep doing it, don't stop . . ."

He had no intentions of stopping, not until she had drained him of every last drop he had to give, and even then he'd continue until his erection subsided . . . and then they would start all over again.

As the sun came up the following morning, Amy Vining and Clint Adams slept a peaceful and exhausted sleep in each other's arms. They had started all over again several times during the night, and finally had drifted off, arms and legs entwined.

On the rise just north of town, Clay Allison checked his gun, and then proceeded to saddle his bay for the ride into town. It would be a short visit, he knew. Once he had done what he came to do, he wouldn't be welcome in Dodge.

He wouldn't want to stay, anyway.

Deputy Sheriff Bill Tilghman lounged in a straight-back chair in front of the jail, with his eyes on the north end of Front Street. He was waiting for a lone rider to come down the street, at which time he would step out and ask the man for his gun, as he was bound to do by city ordinance.

Why waste time, Tilghman thought, waiting for Clay Allison to pick the moment, and then find him? Get it done, get it over with right away. Maybe, by picking the time and place himself, it would give him an edge on the gunman.

Not that he needed one, of course.

Chapter Sixteen

The confrontation between Bill Tilghman and Clay Allison was very straightforward. No one tried to stop it—hell, no one figured they had any right to. It was a man-to-man confrontation, and that's how things were settled in the West. Almost no one would argue that.

"What time is it?" Clint asked, squinting at the light coming through the window.

"Umm, who cares?" Amy replied, burrowing more tightly against him.

"I'm sorry to say that I do," Clint told her. "I've got to get up, honey."

"Ohh—"

"Sorry," he said, sliding out of bed.

Clint pulled on his long underwear, then picked up his pants and padded over to the window.

"Oh, no," he said.

"What is it?"

"Something it looks like I'm too late to stop," he said.

"What?" she said, getting out of bed and wrapping the blanket around her. She came over to stand next to him and peered out the window at Front Street. She saw a man on a bay horse riding down the middle of the street, and another man standing in the street, as if waiting for him.

"What are they doing?" she asked.

"Solving a problem," he said, "the only way they know how."

It was so early that there was practically no one else out. If the confrontation had been taking place later in the day, both sides of the street would have been lined with spectators. Clint could only see a few people, one of whom was Bat Masterson, who was standing right in front of the jail.

"I've got to get out there," Clint said, pulling on his pants.

"Wait for me."

"No, no, you stay here," he said, staggering as he tried to put both boots on at one time.

"I think you're too late," she said.

"I've got to try," he said. "There are other ways for two men to solve a problem."

"What is their problem?" she asked.

"That's hard to say," he replied, strapping on his gun. "They don't know each other."

Clay Allison saw the man standing in the middle of the street, and gave him credit. Tilghman wasn't going to sit still and wait for Allison to find him. Well, that was all right with him. He wanted to get it over with as soon as possible.

"Tilghman?" he asked, stopping his horse.

"That's right, Allison," Tilghman answered. "You're in Dodge City, now. You'll have to give up your gun."

Allison laughed and said, "You'd like that, wouldn't you?"

"I don't like any of this, Allison," Tilghman replied. "Either hand over your gun or turn around and ride out."

"Uh-uh," Allison said. "There's another alternative."

At that point he dismounted and slapped his horse on the rump to get him out of the middle of the street, then turned to face Tilghman.

"If you want my gun, Deputy," Allison said, "you'll have to come and take it."

"Have it your way, Allison."

Tilghman took a step forward. . . .

As Tilghman took one step, Clint Adams came barreling out the front door of the hotel. . . . And as he did, Clay Allison's right hand flashed down for his gun. True to his word, Allison had no intention of allowing the deputy to get close enough to use his fists.

Tilghman was ready for this, however, and as Allison went for his gun, the young lawman did the same, only faster. In his haste, though, and in spite of his confidence, his hurried shot was errant, and instead of striking Allison in the torso, it slammed into his right forearm, rendering the entire arm and hand useless. Allison's gun dropped from the nerveless hand, and he closed his left hand over his wounded arm.

Tilghman actually debated firing again, but couldn't justify it to himself. He leathered his gun and approached Allison, who stared at him with hate-filled eyes.

"Mount up," Tilghman told Allison, "and ride out."

He bent down, picked up the man's gun and put it back in his holster. "If I see you in Dodge again, I'll kill you."

Allison didn't reply. He simply walked to his horse, mounted up with difficulty because of his arm, and then rode back out the way he had come.

Tilghman turned around and his eyes fell on Clint Adams, who was standing in front of the hotel. He stared impassively at the Gunsmith for a few seconds, then averted his eyes and walked to the jail.

The practiced eye of the Gunsmith had recognized that Bill Tilghman's shot had not gone where the young man wanted it to, but he also knew that Tilghman would never admit that fact to anyone.

The confrontation would go down in history, and Tilghman would be lauded for his marksmanship, and mercy.

Chapter Seventeen

For days after the town was buzzing about the confrontation between Tilghman and Clay Allison and, although there had barely been five people on the street to watch it, soon there were dozens of people claiming to have been eyewitnesses to the event.

Clint and Bat were in the Alamo saloon, sitting at the back table, both facing the door.

"Has he talked about it at all?" Clint asked.

"No," Bat said, "but you and I both saw it, we both know what the rest of the town doesn't."

"He's fast," Clint said. "There's no doubt about that, but he rushed his shot. If he'd been up against someone a little faster, or a little more accurate . . ."

"I know," Bat said.

"You're his friend, Bat. Talk to him."

"You can't talk to Bill Tilghman about that," Bat said. "He's going to have to learn all by himself."

"Well, I just hope he doesn't learn the hard way," Clint said. "And dying is a hard way to learn a lesson."

"I can't argue that."

"What's the word on these Texans we're waiting for?"

"Nothing, but from what I hear, Dog Kelly's crew ought to be in some time today."

"I guess we'll just have to wait and see if they're going to mean more trouble, or less. No word yet on who they are?"

"I think Dog wants to surprise us," Bat said, "and by the way, I notice you're using a lot of *we's* and *us's* now."

"Well, hell, I'm here, ain't I?" Clint asked.

"Yeah, you sure are."

They took a moment to order a couple more beers, and then Bat said, "I get the feeling that you're annoyed with me for some reason."

"With you?" Clint asked, looking surprised. "I guess I am sort of annoyed, Bat, but not with you."

"With who, then?"

Clint took a few seconds to examine his feelings, then said, "Tilghman's attitude bothers me."

Shaking his head, Bat said, "Clint, that's the way Bill is—"

"Shouldn't be, Bat," Clint interrupted. "Hickok may have taught Tilghman how to shoot, but somebody should teach him when to use and not to use his hands, whether it be fists or guns."

"Don't you think that might come with age and maturity?"

"At the rate he's going, he may not live that long," Clint said. "No, you can learn when to properly use your gun and when to keep it in your holster at a young age, Bat," Clint explained. "You're proof of that."

"Well, thank you," Bat said, trying to cover the fact that he was indeed very pleased by the praise of the Gunsmith.

"Just stating a fact, Bat. It can be done, and someone has to teach Bill Tilghman that."

"You?"

"I might as well do something constructive while I'm here," Clint reasoned.

"Tilghman is hard to teach anything to," Bat said. "Maybe that's because his first teacher *was* Wild Bill Hickok."

"That could be," Clint said. "It would be hard for anyone else to measure up to Bill."

"But you're going to try?"

"Somebody has to. He certainly has the confidence and the ability, but he's got to lose that cockiness, or he's going to lose something a lot more dear to him."

Chapter Eighteen

When Dog Kelly's help finally arrived, there were three, and simply by riding down Front Street, they created some excitement.

Someone ran into the Alamo saloon and announced very loudly that the men had arrived, and both Clint and Bat made their way to the street to take a look-see, and were very pleasantly surprised.

"I'll be damned!" was the way Bat Masterson put it, and the Gunsmith was struck speechless.

The man riding just ahead of the other two rode tall in the saddle, clad in a dark suit and a flat-brim dark hat. His name was Wyatt Earp, and he was not only responding to the call for help put out by Dog Kelly, but to a wire that he had received from the elected mayor of Dodge City, George Hoover.

Riding behind him were the two men he had persuaded to come with him. One was Neal Brown, a handy man with a gun who had little or no reputation for it, and the other was Ed Masterson, brother of Bat, who knew how to handle a gun and had worked as a lawman before.

"That's your brother riding with Wyatt, isn't it?" Clint asked. He had met Ed Masterson briefly, soon after he had met Bat, when Ed and Wyatt's brothers had ridden into Deadman's Flats to bail Wyatt, Bat and Clint out of a tight spot.*

"It sure is," Bat said, grinning from ear to ear. "Been awhile since I seen Ed."

"It's been awhile since I've seen Wyatt," Clint said. "He looks good."

"Yeah, they all look good," Bat said. "Who's that other fella riding with them?"

"I don't know," Clint said, "but if he's with Wyatt and Ed, he must be okay. Let's get their horses taken care of, Bat."

"Right. They're bound to be thirsty."

Bat grabbed a couple of youngsters who were standing nearby and told them to come with him, and then followed Clint out into the street to meet his brother.

When Wyatt Earp saw Clint Adams standing in the center of the street he pulled his horse to a stop and stared at the Gunsmith.

"Hell," he said, "if you're here, what the hell did they need me for?"

"Hello, Wyatt," Clint said, stepping forward and extending his hand.

"Clint, you look good," Wyatt said.

"So do you," Clint responded. "You filled out some since the last time I saw you. Look a little older too."

"You don't look a day older than the last time I saw

*The Gunsmith #5: Three Guns for Glory

you," Wyatt replied, "but I still wouldn't want to ever get as old as you are."

"Step down off that horse, sonny," Clint said, "and we'll have somebody take care of it for you."

"Like who?" Wyatt asked, but when he looked past Clint and saw Bat he smiled and stepped down. "Bat Masterson. Finally found a job that suits you, eh, boy?"

"Step aside, Earp, and let me greet my brother," Bat said.

He patted Wyatt on the shoulder as he passed him, then embraced his brother, who affectionately referred to him as "Billy."

"Better sit on that name while you're in Dodge, Ed," Bat said, explaining about Bill Tilghman being the other deputy.

"Tilghman?" Wyatt said, turning to face Bat. "Is that the fella we heard put the boots to Clay Allison a few days ago?"

"The same," Bat said. "Come on, you boys, take these horses over to the livery and get them tended to."

"Come on, Wyatt," Clint said. "We'll go over to the Alhambra and wash away some of that trail dust."

"Suits me," Wyatt said. "Is that Kelly's place?"

"It is."

"Well, we'll go anyway."

The three men gave up their mounts, and then walked to the saloon with Clint and Bat.

Once they were firmly entrenched at a back table with a beer each, Wyatt introduced Neal Brown and assured Clint and Bat that the man was extremely able with a gun, and would pull his weight in any kind of situation.

"That's good enough for us," Bat said. "Welcome, Neal."

"You plan on reporting to Kelly?" Clint asked.

"Hell, no," Wyatt said. "I didn't come here from Wichita in response to the call of a saloon owner. Mayor Hoover sent me a wire saying he wanted me to take over the job of town marshal."

"Marshal?" Clint asked, looking at Bat. "I know the county sheriff's in Dodge—that's Charlie Bassett—but I didn't know this town had a marshal."

"I guess that tells you why Hoover wants to replace him," Bat said. He turned to Wyatt and said, "I'm glad to hear that, Wyatt."

"So am I. I brought Ed and Neal to act as my deputies. There's a job for you, too, Bat, if you want it."

"I think I'll hang on to this star for a while, Wyatt," Bat said, touching his deputy's badge.

"Job's there when you want it," Wyatt assured him. He did not offer a job to Clint Adams, however, as much as he would have liked to have Clint as a deputy, because he knew how the Gunsmith felt about ever wearing a badge again.

Wyatt finished his beer and then stood up, saying, "Well, I guess I'll check in with Hoover. Ed, you and Neal might as well stay right here. I'll pick up your badges and then swear you in myself."

"Fine with me," Ed said. "I'm ready for another beer."

"So am I," Brown chimed in.

"We'll keep them right here for you," Bat said, laying his hand affectionately on his brother's forearm.

"I'm sure of that," Wyatt said. "Bat, I'm looking forward to meeting Bill Tilghman."

"He'll be around, Wyatt," Bat assured his friend. "Don't worry about that."

"Wyatt, you mind if I walk over to the mayor's office with you?" Clint asked.

"I don't mind, Clint. I welcome your company."

"I'll see you fellas later," Clint said, getting to his feet.

"Stay sober, boys," Wyatt warned his two future deputies.

Clint and Wyatt left the Alhambra together, and once they were out on the street Wyatt asked, "What's on your mind, Clint?"

"What makes you think something's on my mind?"

"I haven't seen you in quite a while, but I can still tell when something is bothering you. What is it?"

"It's Tilghman," Clint answered, and then went on to explain why the young deputy was weighing heavily on his mind.

"I'd think he'd be glad to take some advice from you," Wyatt said afterward.

"According to Bat, Tilghman doesn't take advice from anyone. You weren't planning to offer him a job too, were you?"

"I hadn't thought about it," Wyatt said. "I don't know him so, no, I don't think I'm ready to offer Bill Tilghman a job."

"All right," Clint said. He didn't think Tilghman was ready to take on the responsibility of being a deputy marshal, and he was glad that Wyatt had no immediate plans to offer him the job.

"If he impresses me while I'm here I might change my mind, though," Wyatt added.

"That sounds fair enough," Clint replied.

"What about you, Clint?" Wyatt asked. "How have you been?"

"All right, I suppose," Clint said.

"I heard some things about you back when Hickok was killed," Wyatt said.

"They were probably true, Wyatt," Clint said. "I went through a bad time, but I straightened out."

"Good, I'm glad," Wyatt said as they stopped in front of the city hall. "You know why I didn't offer you a job, Clint, but it's there if you want it."

"You've got some good deputies, Wyatt," Clint said, "but I'll be around to help—unofficially—if you should need it."

"Good, I'm glad to hear that," Wyatt said. "Do you want to come in with me?"

"No need for that," Clint said. "I guess I'll go back to the saloon. Maybe we can get up a poker game."

"Neal's not much of a gambler, but you'll have to watch out for Ed. He's as bad—or as good—as Bat."

"I'll keep it in mind," Clint said. He shook Wyatt's hand again and said, "It's really good to see you again, Wyatt. You're making quite a name for yourself."

"You know what that's like, Clint," Earp said.

"Yes," Clint said soberly. "I do."

Clint waited until Wyatt went inside, then turned and headed back for the Alhambra. Maybe, he thought, with Wyatt's influence now in Dodge, they could all join forces and straighten Bill Tilghman out.

Before somebody laid him out.

Chapter Nineteen

Hoover was ecstatic to see Wyatt Earp in his office, and made no bones about it.

"Marshal Earp," he said, rising from his desk and rushing forward to greet Wyatt.

"Not quite yet, Mr. Mayor."

"We can take care of that immediately, don't worry about that," Mayor Hoover said.

He went back around his desk and took the marshal's badge out of his desk drawer. He handed it to Wyatt and very quickly went through the swearing-in ceremony, then congratulated *Marshal* Earp.

"I can't tell you how relieved I am to see that badge pinned to your shirt, Marshal," Hoover said.

"I don't really understand what you've been so concerned about, Mayor," Wyatt said, securing the badge to his chest. "Just in the few minutes I've been in town I've seen two men who could probably handle these problems you're expecting very nicely."

"Oh? Have you met the sheriff and his deputies?"

"One of his deputies, Bat Masterson, is a good friend of mine," Wyatt said. "I'd trust him with my life, but no, I haven't yet met Sheriff Bassett and his other deputy, Bill Tilghman."

"Oh? Then who is the other man you spoke of?"

"Clint Adams," Wyatt said, and when Hoover frowned, attempting to place the name, the new marshal added, "Some folks call him the Gunsmith."

"The Gunsmith?" Hoover asked. "Here in my town? I had no idea! But that's wonderful. You can make him one of your deputies—"

"No chance," Wyatt said, interrupting the mayor. "He would never accept the job."

"I don't understand. I understood that he was a lawman—"

"He used to be a damned good one, but he doesn't wear a badge anymore."

"That's a shame."

"Yes, it is, but Clint and I are also friends, and if something comes up where I need him, he'll be there, as a private citizen."

"How long will he be in town?"

"I don't know that for sure," Wyatt said, "but if he's here, he'll help."

"Well, do you have any deputies in mind?"

"I brought two men with me. Neal Brown and Ed Masterson, both very good men."

"Masterson?"

"Yes, Bat's brother. I offered Bat a job also, but he prefers to remain as one of Bassett's deputies for the time being."

"Then you'll be needing two deputy's badges," the

mayor said, once again dipping into his drawer and coming up with two tin stars. He handed them to Wyatt, who put them both in his shirt pocket.

"Now, Mr. Mayor, why don't you tell me exactly what the problem is that you're expecting."

"Just what I said in my wire, Marshal. We've heard that a large number of Texans are heading for Dodge."

"And what are their intentions?"

The mayor spread his hands helplessly and shook his head. "We don't know for sure." He went on to tell Wyatt the story of Bill Tilghman's confrontation with Texas Bill, and finished by saying, "Perhaps they're planning some sort of reprisal for that incident. I simply don't feel that this bodes well for our town."

"Well, I guess we'll just have to wait and see what develops," Wyatt said. "I wouldn't worry, though, Mr. Mayor. We have enough able men here now to handle the problem."

"I'm glad to hear that, Marshal," Hoover said, seating himself heavily behind his desk. "I don't mind telling you that just having you here makes me feel much better."

"We'll try to justify your confidence, Mayor. I'll coordinate my efforts with Sheriff Bassett, and his deputies. I'm sure we'll be able to handle anything that comes along."

"We have a lot of confidence in our sheriff and his deputies," Hoover was quick to add, "but both deputies *are* very young, you know."

"Well, I can't speak for Tilghman," Wyatt said, "but Bat is wise beyond his years, and I've heard some good things about Tilghman."

And, he added to himself, remembering what Clint had told him, *some bad*.

"Still and all, I'm glad you're here."

Before the mayor could repeat how pleased he was again, Wyatt said, "I'll just see about swearing in my deputies and then I'll talk to the sheriff."

"Very well," the mayor said.

Wyatt touched the brim of his hat and left the mayor's office to return to the Alhambra saloon.

Chapter Twenty

When Wyatt returned to the saloon he found Clint, Bat, Ed and Neal all taking part in a friendly poker game. It was simply a way for them to pass the time while Clint and Bat got acquainted with Neal, and Bat and Ed caught up on what had been happening since they'd last seen each other.

Wyatt stopped at the bar to get himself a beer, and then joined them at the table.

"Sitting in?" Bat asked.

"Why not?" he asked, reaching into his shirt pocket. "I'll open with these," he said, tossing a badge in front of Ed and Neal. "You boys consider yourselves sworn in. Bat, you and Clint are witnesses."

"Right," he said, and Clint simply nodded while shuffling the cards.

"How'd you like our mayor?" Bat asked.

"About as much as I like any politician," Wyatt

answered, "but he wasn't too bad. I just wanted to get out of his office before he kissed me."

"That glad to see you, huh?" Bat asked.

"Extremely pleased would be putting it mildly," Wyatt said.

Clint had dealt out five hands of draw poker, and all of them spread their cards out to look at them.

"I'm afraid our mayor is a little concerned about me and Tilghman being so young," Bat said, adding, "as if that was our fault. I open for a dollar."

Everybody chipped in their dollar and Wyatt said, "When do I get to meet this Tilghman, the man who outdrew Clay Allison?"

"You start calling him that and it isn't going to do him any good," Clint said.

Wyatt looked at Bat, who shrugged and said, "You'll meet Tilghman soon enough. I'll take two cards."

They took two or three cards, and when it came around to Clint he dealt himself one.

"Bat, do you know where Sheriff Bassett is?" Wyatt asked.

"Probably in his office," Bat said, examining his cards. "I'll bet ten dollars, boys."

They called him around the table, and then he laid down three pretty queens accompanied by two lowly deuces. "Full house."

"Still up to your old tricks, huh, Bat?" Wyatt asked, throwing in his hand.

"I don't know what you mean," Bat said. "I didn't deal, Clint did."

"And quite well too," Clint said. He laid down his cards, showing three kings and two threes.

"You took one card," Bat said, aghast. "That's crazy."

"It's only for fun, isn't it?" Clint asked, raking in the pot.

"Poker is never for fun," Bat said, throwing his hands up in disgust.

"Oh, I don't know," Wyatt said. "The look on your face right now is pretty funny."

Wyatt stood up as the cards were gathered up for another deal and said, "I'm going to go and talk to the sheriff. You gentlemen will excuse me, won't you?"

"With your attitude," Bat Masterson said, "you don't belong in a poker game, anyway."

Chapter Twenty-One

About a half an hour after Wyatt Earp left, Clint Adams decided to take his leave too. Being there with the Masterson brothers and Neal Brown, Clint found so much youthful exuberance was making him feel very old.

When he got to his room, he found someone even younger waiting for him.

"Hi," Amy said from his bed.

"Hello, Amy," he said. He closed the door behind him and added, "This isn't very discreet, is it?"

"I don't really care, Clint," she said. "But I was careful. I came in the back way. It wasn't locked."

"I see."

Clint wasn't one to hesitate when he found a beautiful, desirable woman in his bed—and it had happened a few times before—but he wasn't feeling up to par tonight, and knowing that Amy was only nineteen didn't help either. She should have been in Tilghman's bed, or one of the Mastersons', not his.

"What's wrong, Clint?" she asked, noticing the look on his face. "Aren't you glad to see me?"

"Sure," he said, moving towards the bed. "Sure I'm glad to see you, Amy."

"Then why don't you look glad?" she asked, frowning. Suddenly, something occurred to her which frightened her.

Had he gotten all that he wanted from her the other night? Was that why she hadn't heard from him these past couple of days?

"I think I understand—" she said. She threw the covers back and swung her legs to the floor, preparing to get up.

"Wait," Clint said, realizing what she must have been thinking. "Wait a minute, Amy," he said, sitting next to her. "You're wrong."

"Am I?"

"Yes, you are," he said, putting a hand on her shoulder. He suddenly became very aware that she was totally naked, and his pulse quickened.

"Amy—"

"What's wrong, Clint?" she asked. "I thought you liked me, really liked me."

"I do," he assured her.

"Then I'm confused," she said. "I thought you'd be very glad to see me here tonight."

"Amy, I am," he said. "It's just that—"

"What?"

"You're so young," he said, cupping her chin in his hand.

"Is that what's bothering you?" she asked. "It's because I'm nineteen?"

"And I'm considerably more than nineteen."

"That doesn't matter to me, Clint," she said, "so it

shouldn't matter to you. I don't expect anything from you. That's not what you're afraid of, is it? That I'm so young and foolish that I expect you to marry me or something?"

"No, of course not—"

"Then stop talking," she said. She grabbed his hand and laid it over her right breast. "Stop talking and stop thinking. I'm not asking you to love me," she told him, "just to make love to me . . . now! Please!"

There was such a cloud over her face that he actually felt that he had to do as she asked . . . but aside from that, he suddenly found that he wanted to, very much.

He leaned over to kiss her, and she threw her arms around his neck and mashed her lips tightly against his. She opened her mouth then and thrust her tongue into his, and he pushed her back on the bed and massaged her breasts while they kissed.

"Get undressed," she whispered to him. "Hurry!"

He quickly shucked his clothes and climbed back into bed with her. The reason for his hesitancy was gone. In fact, reason was gone, and only need remained, for both of them.

Clint pressed his face against her breasts, inhaling the clean, fresh scent of her, and his hand strayed between her legs. She moaned in response to his touch, and when he began to suckle her nipples while he manipulated her with his fingers, her body was racked by a tremendous orgasm which left her panting, but begging for more.

He slid his thigh over hers, then moved over her. She took hold of his penis and guided it through the damp forest of her pubic thatch and deep inside of her.

"Oh, God," she cried, raising her hips up off the bed. "Oh please . . ."

He held her tightly to him and worked himself

feverishly in and out of her, until they were both racked by violent tremors, and his semen exploded from him and filled her with tiny needles of fire.

Chapter Twenty-Two

The next morning there was a meeting of all of the Dodge City lawmen in the office of Sheriff Charlie Bassett. Wyatt Earp did not wish to alienate Bassett at all, which was why he called for the meeting in Bassett's office instead of his own. The Gunsmith was invited to sit in on the meeting.

"Why is Adams here?" Bassett asked.

"I invited him," Wyatt replied. He didn't feel the need to explain himself, but again he wanted the man to feel at ease. He did not want to create an adversary relationship between himself and the town sheriff. "He's here unofficially."

"I offered him a job and he turned me down," Bassett said, sounding petulant.

"I know," Wyatt said. "I made him the same offer, and he turned me down too. Still, he's been kind enough to offer his help, without the benefit of wearing a badge. Any objections?"

Bassett grumbled, but said no.

"Good. Gentlemen, this is going to be a short meeting. I just wanted us all to meet and agree on total cooperation with one another. As I understand it, this town is expecting some trouble, and we've been asked to come in and help out."

"Suits me," Bat said.

"I think we could have handled it ourselves," Tilghman said.

"You would," Clint said, and Tilghman gave him a quick look.

They got the introductions out of the way and Wyatt said, "I just want this to be a cordial working relationship. None of us has to be friends, we just have to be able to work together."

"My men will cooperate," Bassett said.

"Fine," Wyatt said. "Then that's it."

As the men were filing out of the office, Clint approached Wyatt and said, "I'm hurt."

"About what?"

"You didn't introduce me."

"Everybody knows you, Clint," Wyatt said. "Besides, you're not official, remember?"

"Yeah."

Bassett started walking past them and Wyatt said, "Are you going out, Sheriff?"

"Yes, I am. I have some work to do."

"Would you mind if I used your office for a minute?"

"What for?"

"I want to talk to one of your men."

Bassett flipped his hand and said, "Be my guest. We gotta cooperate, right?"

"That's right, Sheriff."

The sheriff nodded, and then left.

"Who are you going to talk to?" Clint asked. "Tilghman?"

"Who else?"

"About what?"

Wyatt shrugged. "I don't know him. I just want to make sure he knows me. Don't worry, I won't tell him you said anything about him to me."

"Do whatever you think you have to do, Wyatt. You want me to send him back in?"

"Yeah, please."

"Okay, I'll see you later."

Clint stepped outside and found Bat and Tilghman standing there, talking.

"Tilghman."

"Yeah?" the young deputy said, turning to face him.

"The marshal would like to talk to you inside," he said.

"About what?"

Clint shrugged and said, "Maybe you'd better go inside and find out."

Tilghman looked at Bat, who also shrugged, then stepped past Clint into the sheriff's office.

"What's that all about?" Bat asked.

"I think Wyatt just wants to clear the air."

"I think we'd better stick around."

"Why?"

"Tilghman's a hothead," Bat said, "you know that. Whatever Wyatt's going to tell him, I don't know how he's going to take it."

"You think they're going to go at each other?"

"They might," Bat said, "and to tell you the truth, Clint, I wouldn't want to bet on the outcome."

Chapter Twenty-Three

As it turned out, the meeting and the outcome were very peaceful, and when the door to the jail opened and Tilghman stepped out, Bat let out a breath he must have been holding the whole time.

Clint had been surprised by Bat's remark about not betting on the outcome. Of course, he had not known Tilghman as long as Bat had, but from what he had seen, he would not place the young deputy in the same class as Wyatt Earp. It was interesting—and puzzling—to him that Bat Masterson would.

"What was it about?" Bat asked Tilghman.

"Not much," Tilghman said. "The marshal just wanted to make sure I knew what I was doing."

"Meaning what?"

"He heard about Texas Bill and Clay Allison. He just wondered if I made a habit of solving my problems that way."

"What way?" Bat asked. "You didn't have much choice in either one of those cases."

"Really?" Tilghman said. "Is that the way you feel, Bat?"

"Why wouldn't I?"

"Well, you're the one who keeps telling me I'm hotheaded," Tilghman said. "You sure you didn't tell your friend Wyatt Earp the same thing? He thinks I'm going to go for my gun first chance I get!"

"Hey, wait a minute!" Bat said. "I never told Wyatt anything about you, Bill."

"Uh-huh. Then tell me why—"

"Hold on," Clint said. Obviously Tilghman had jumped to a totally wrong conclusion, and he had to set it straight before a rift formed between the two young men. "Bat never said a word to Wyatt, Tilghman."

"Oh, yeah?" Tilghman said, turning to face Clint. "Then that means it must have been you, right?"

"That's right," Clint said.

"What gives you the right, Adams?" Tilghman demanded. "What makes you an authority on Bill Tilghman?"

"I'm not, Bill," Clint said, "but I have noticed some things about you that—"

"Something you felt you just had to pass on to the new marshal, right? This way he won't offer me a job as one of his deputies, right?"

"Is that what you want?"

"Of course, that's what I want," Tilghman snapped. "I want to be a lawman—"

"Then prove yourself worthy," Clint said, interrupting him. "Show Wyatt that you can do the job, and that you can exercise restraint when you have to."

"Restraint," Tilghman repeated, shaking his head derisively.

"Restraint is one of a lawman's most important weapons," Clint said, "and the knowledge, the instinctive knowledge of when to use it and when to cast it aside."

"Sure, spoken like a true lawman," Tilghman said. "Tell me, Adams, why aren't you wearing a badge anymore? Did it get too heavy for you?"

"Sure, Bill," Clint said, "it got too heavy. Look, you don't have any problems here. Just prove to the marshal that—"

"Forget it, Adams," Tilghman said. "I don't need any words of advice from you, now or ever. Wyatt Earp will find out soon enough what kind of a lawman I am."

Tilghman turned away to look at Bat for a moment, then he turned and walked away from both of them.

"If you ever had any hope of teaching him anything . . ." Bat said, but he let it trail off, because Clint Adams knew exactly what he meant.

Chapter Twenty-Four

Bat and Clint were having lunch in the Dodge House dining room—and not being served by Maggie Lane—when Neal Brown came rushing in.

"Bat!"

"What's up, Neal?"

"Plenty," Neal said. "Wes Hardin is in town, and he's over at the Alhambra."

"Wes Hardin?" Clint said.

"Wyatt wanted me to let everyone know that Hardin was here," Neal Brown said.

"Does he want any kind of action taken?"

"Just for everyone to be aware."

"Have you told Tilghman yet?" Clint asked.

"Not yet. I haven't found him."

"Tell Wyatt that we'll pass the information on to Tilghman ourselves," Clint said.

"All right," Neal said. "Have you seen Ed, Bat?"

"Not today."

"I'll find him," he said. "See you fellas later."

"Right."

As he left, Clint fell deep into thought and Bat snapped his fingers in front of his friend's face and said, "Hey, come back."

"This is going to be a problem," Clint said.

"How so?"

"Tilghman."

"What about him?"

"Don't you see? This is going to look to him like his chance to impress Wyatt."

"By facing Wes Hardin?"

"What was your first thought when Neal told us Wes Hardin was at the Alhambra?"

"To go over there," Bat said. "I see what you mean."

"You resisted the impulse," Clint pointed out, "but do you think Tilghman will?"

"Not a chance."

"He'll get himself killed, and then one of us will have to kill Hardin. That will be two unnecessary deaths, and maybe more if we try to take Hardin out of the saloon. Tilghman could start lead flying in that crowded saloon, and who knows how many people may end up dead."

"I see what you mean."

"I've got to talk to Hardin."

"Now who's being impulsive?"

"No, I mean just talk to him," Clint said, "although I admit it won't be easy. I'm not exactly one of his favorite people."

"You know Wes Hardin?" Bat asked, surprised.

"Yeah, we met once before, in Abilene," Clint said. "It was a weird thing, Bat. Hickok seemed to see something in Hardin, maybe a little of himself, and they became friends."

"What's wrong with that?"

"Nothing, I guess," the Gunsmith said. "But Hardin's a killer, and Bill just seemed to refuse to see that."

"Hardin was very young then."

"He's about your age," Clint said. "Yours and Tilghman's. The three of you, you're all so young."

"Yeah, but like I said before, that's not our fault, is it?" Bat asked.

"No, it isn't," Clint said, "but I want to try and make sure that you all get a little older—even Wes."

As Clint started to get up Bat said, "Let me go with you."

"No," Clint said. "What you've got to do is locate Tilghman and keep him away from the Alhambra until I get rid of Hardin."

"Get rid of him?" Bat asked. "And just how do you intend to work that magic?"

"Easy," Clint said. "I'm simply going to convince him that it would not be in his best interests to stay."

"Uh, Neal did say that Wyatt didn't want anyone to take any kind of action," Bat reminded him.

"See?" Clint said. "Already I've got an advantage over you because I'm not wearing a badge. You're bound by Wyatt's word, but I'm not."

Chapter Twenty-Five

Clint and Wes Hardin had disliked each other almost immediately upon meeting, and Clint didn't feel that four years would have changed that. Even now, as he approached the saloon, he felt his insides tensing up. There had been a moment in Abilene when, had it not been for Hickok's intervention, either the Gunsmith or Wes Hardin would have died. Hickok had stepped between them, and that had been the last time Clint saw Hardin.*

When Clint walked through the batwing doors of the Alhambra he noticed that the volume of noise was not as loud as it usually was. It wasn't hard to guess why. Hardin's presence was having a dampening effect on the normal mood of the place. There was tremendous tension in the air, and he wondered how long it would be before somebody decided to try and do something about it.

The Gunsmith #4: The Guns of Abilene

Wes Hardin's presence was a danger to the whole town, and he had to get him to leave without Hardin taking it as a challenge.

Clint walked to the bar and noticed that Neal Brown had found his way back to the Alhambra. He was standing at the end of the bar, and by following his line of vision, Clint was able to locate Hardin, sitting at a back table with a bottle of whiskey. The man had changed a lot in four years. He had filled out, although he wasn't a big man by any means.

Clint moved down to the end of the bar and caught Neal Brown's attention.

"What are you doing here?" the deputy asked.

"I'm going to talk to Hardin," Clint said.

"Wait a minute," Brown said. "Wyatt don't want anybody doing anything—"

"He doesn't want any of the *deputies* doing anything," Clint cut in. "I'm not a deputy, Neal. Besides, Hardin and I know each other. I want to try and get him to leave town before something happens."

"If we keep an eye on him, nothing will happen."

"Maybe so," Clint said, "but I've got a real bad feeling about this, and I've got to do something before somebody gets killed."

"I can't let you—"

"You can't stop me," Clint said. "Just stay here and watch, okay?"

Clint turned to the bar and ordered a beer. When he had it in his hand he looked at Brown and said, "Here goes."

"I still don't like it," Brown said. "Maybe I should go and get Wyatt."

"Maybe you should," Clint said, and started towards Wes Hardin's table. When some of the people in the saloon realized where he was headed, they stopped what they were doing to watch. The young killer, sensing the change in the atmosphere, looked up just as Clint reached the table.

"Hello, Hardin," Clint greeted.

Wes Hardin stared up at Clint's face, frowning. He wasn't trying to place the Gunsmith, he was simply trying to adjust himself to the fact that he was there.

"Adams," he finally said.

"You mind if I sit down?"

Hardin spread his hands and said, "I don't mind."

Hardin was seated with his back to the wall, so Clint took the other chair nearest the wall and then turned it so that he was facing the door.

"Still careful," Hardin said.

"Still alive, anyway," Clint said.

"You're not wearing a star."

"No, I'm not. I'm just passing through. Got a couple of friends in town. Maybe you heard of them."

"Who?"

"Wyatt Earp. Bat and Ed Masterson."

Hardin hesitated a moment, then said, "Yeah, seems to me I may have heard those names around. Interesting friends."

"Yeah, very interesting," Clint said, "and something else is interesting too."

"Oh, yeah? What's that?"

"They're wearing badges."

"All of them?"

"Yeah, all of them . . . and more."

"Sounds like a stacked deck," Hardin said.

"It is."

Hardin nodded and poured himself another shot of

whiskey. Clint filled in the time by drinking his beer.

"What's on your mind, Adams?"

"You," Clint said. "I don't want anybody in this town to die."

"You looking for miracles now? Everybody's got to die sometime, Adams. You know that. A good friend of yours died a while back."

Clint knew who he meant. "Hickok."

"Yeah, Hickok," Hardin said. "Wild Bill."

"He was your friend too."

"I don't have any friends, Adams," Hardin said. "You know what happens if you have a lot of friends? Sooner or later you've got to kill some of them."

"In your world, maybe."

"You're in a different world than me, Mr. Gunsmith?" Hardin asked viciously. "I'd be willing to bet that you killed more men than I have. Want to count?"

"No," Clint said. "Counting is your game, not mine. You may know exactly how many men you've killed, Hardin, but I don't want you adding to that count here in Dodge."

"You telling me to leave town?" Hardin asked, narrowing his eyes.

"No, I'm not telling you anything," Clint said. "You'd like that. You'd take that as a challenge."

Hardin sipped his whiskey and didn't reply.

"I'm making a suggestion," Clint went on. "I'm suggesting that it's foolish to buck a stacked deck. I'm suggesting that maybe you should go and find another game."

"Another game," Hardin repeated.

"Think about it, Wes," Clint said. "That's all I'm asking. This town has got enough trouble coming its way without adding you to the list.''

"Oh, yeah," Hardin said. "I heard about that. Big group of Texans on the way, right?''

"Yeah, that's right.''

"Just like Abilene.''

"I hope not," Clint said. "Do you know anything about this?''

"Just what I hear," Hardin said.

"What did you hear?''

"I heard what you heard, nothing more," Hardin said. He poured himself another shot of whiskey, leaving about another shot's worth left in the bottle.

"You got something else to say?" Hardin asked.

"Just this," Clint replied. "Think about what I said— and remember: I take care of my friends.''

"Now that," Hardin said, "sounds like a challenge.''

"You can take it any way you want, Wes," Clint said. "I hate acting like a hardcase, and I hate using my gun, but I take care of my friends.''

Clint stood up, leaving his empty mug on the table next to Hardin's bottle.

"I believe you, Adams," Hardin said.

"What's it going to be, then?''

Hardin shrugged and said, "When my bottle is as empty as your glass I'll decide.''

Clint was tempted to upend the bottle and pour what was left on the floor, but that *would* be a challenge. He decided to let Hardin make up his mind on his own.

Clint went back to the bar and stood where Neal Brown had been. He hadn't seen Brown leave, but he'd probably gone to get Wyatt Earp.

"Another beer," he told the bartender.

When he got the beer he deliberately kept his back to

Hardin so the young gunman wouldn't think he was watching him. That was why he didn't see Bill Tilghman enter the saloon.

"Hardin!" Tilghman's voice rang out suddenly.

When Clint turned he looked at Hardin first, and then at Tilghman. The young gunman hadn't moved, but he was looking at the doorway where the lawman stood.

"Damn," Clint muttered under his breath. He was too far from Tilghman to do anything, unless he used his gun, and he didn't want to do that.

Hardin peered at Tilghman and when he saw the badge on his chest he said, "Are you talking to me, Deputy?"

"Yeah, I'm talking to you, Hardin," Tilghman said. "I want you to get out of Dodge City . . . now!"

"Is that a fact?"

"That's right, it is," Tilghman said. Clint could see the tension in the deputy's shoulders, and his wide-spread legs. Hardin, on the other hand, was totally relaxed.

Clint was convinced that Tilghman was going to get himself killed, and if that happened it would force him into action, also.

"Tilghman—" he began, but the deputy cut him off.

"Don't get in my way, Adams!"

"I don't want to get in your way, Deputy," Clint said. "All I want to do is keep you alive."

"You better worry about this two-bit killer, Adams, not me," Tilghman advised.

"I've already talked to Hardin," Clint said. "There's no need for you to do this."

"I'm the law here, Adams, not you," Tilghman reminded him. "You gave up wearing a badge, remember?"

"That has nothing to do with this—"

"Just mind your own business, Adams," Tilghman said. "Hardin, are you leaving?"

"Well," Hardin drawled, pouring the last of the whiskey into his glass, "I was planning on leaving, but I may have just changed my mind."

"That would be unfortunate for you," Tilghman said.

"It will be unfortunate for someone, that's for sure," Hardin replied. "Just who will be up to you."

Hardin tilted back his glass to drain it, and Clint knew that when he finished his drink he would stand up. At that moment, Tilghman would go for his gun, and one of them would die.

And he was helpless to stop it.

"Tilghman—" Clint shouted, stepping forward, but he knew he'd be too late. Hardin was standing up and Tilghman's right arm was tensing. He heard Hardin's chair scrape against the floor, and Tilghman's hand started to move—

At that moment Wyatt Earp stepped through the batwing doors and brought the butt of his gun down on Bill Tilghman's head. The deputy fell to the floor, and his gun dropped from his hand.

Bat Masterson and Neal Brown stepped in behind Wyatt and the marshal said, "Get him out of here," pointing down at Tilghman.

Between them Bat and Brown lifted Tilghman up and carried him out. Wyatt bent over, picked up Tilghman's fallen gun, and tucked it into his belt.

"As I understood it, Mr. Hardin," he said then, addressing the young gunman who was now standing, "you were about to leave?"

Hardin looked at Clint, then back at Marshal Earp and said, "I only came into town for a drink, Marshal. My intention all along was to leave when I finished."

"I suggest you do so, then."

Hardin looked over at Clint again, and it was as if some sort of message passed between them. Clint knew that Hardin wasn't leaving because he was afraid of Wyatt or of Clint. It was something else, and the only connection between him and the gunman was Wild Bill Hickok.

Wes Hardin had not admitted to his friendship with Hickok, but Clint had a feeling that if they each had not had that as part of their past, Hardin wouldn't be leaving so easily.

A favor, his eyes were telling Clint, and the Gunsmith nodded his acceptance of it, and his thanks.

Hardin stepped around his table and started for the door. When he reached Earp they were face to face, and the marshal stepped aside to allow the younger man to leave.

"Am I glad you came when you did," Clint said, approaching Wyatt.

"Neal came by and told me what you were up to," Wyatt replied. Clint could see that he was angry, but that he was trying to control himself. "Could we step outside, please?"

"Sure, Wyatt."

The two men stepped out onto the boardwalk and Wyatt said, "I left instructions for no one to make a move on Wes Hardin."

"First of all, I'm not one of your deputies, subject to your instructions," Clint pointed out, "and secondly, I did not make a move on Hardin."

"What do you call it?"

"I was having a drink with the man," Clint said. "We were discussing old times."

"Old times?"

Clint outlined briefly his last—and first—meeting with John Wesley Hardin.

"What old times did you discuss, then?" Wyatt asked. "How you almost killed one another?"

"No," Clint said. "We discussed Bill Hickok . . . and playing against a stacked deck."

Chapter Twenty-Six

Bat and Neal Brown had carried Bill Tilghman to the marshal's office, where he was now sitting on a cot in one of the cells, rubbing his head.

"Who hit me?" he demanded.

"I did," Wyatt said.

Tilghman looked up and saw who was speaking, and then said, "But why?"

"Because you were about to get yourself killed."

"Killed?" Tilghman snapped, standing up quickly—too quickly, as he staggered briefly before regaining his balance. "Hardin is the one who would have been killed—"

"And that would have been even worse," Wyatt said, cutting him off.

"What?"

"What the hell did you think you were trying to do?" the marshal demanded. "Didn't you get my instructions?"

Tilghman didn't like being called on the carpet, especially since Clint was there to see it, as well as the other deputies. The only one who wasn't there was Charlie Bassett.

"Bat did say something—"

"Bat gave you my instructions and you still went over there to make a grandstand play?" Wyatt demanded.

"I wasn't making a grandstand play," Tilghman retorted. "I was upholding the law."

"You don't even believe that," Wyatt said.

Tilghman looked disgusted and rubbed the back of his head. "Are you going to tell Charlie?"

Wyatt frowned for a moment and Bat said, "He means Sheriff Bassett."

"Bassett," Wyatt said. "Uh, yeah, I'm going to tell Bassett, because it's better for you that he hears it from me rather than from some cowboy who was in the saloon tonight."

"He'll take my badge," Tilghman said.

"No," Wyatt said. "I'll recommend that he doesn't take your badge."

Tilghman looked up and asked, "Why would you do that?"

"Because I think you've got the makings of a good lawman," Wyatt said, "and so do Bat and Clint, and I respect their judgment."

Clint flinched when Wyatt mentioned his name, because he knew that it would not endear him to Tilghman, not the way the young man felt about him already.

He looked at the deputy, but Tilghman was staring at the floor.

"How's your head?" Wyatt asked.

"Huh? Oh, it's fine."

"Yeah, sure," the marshal said. "Bat, why don't you take Bill over to the doc and get him checked out. After that, you fellas can continue on your rounds."

"Right, Wyatt," Bat said. He walked to Tilghman's side and helped him up and out of the office.

"What do you think?" Wyatt asked the rest of the people in the office.

Ed Masterson answered first. "I can only go by what you say," he remarked, "and I'd go along with your decision, Wyatt. Don't let Bassett take his star."

"Neal?"

Neal Brown shrugged and said, "I don't know him, so I'll just go along with you too."

Wyatt turned to Clint, who shrugged helplessly. "He won't listen to me, so maybe you can straighten him out."

"I've got enough things to do," Wyatt said, "but I guess I can give it a try."

"Fine," Clint said, getting to his feet.

"You talked Hardin into leaving, didn't you?" Wyatt asked.

"I don't know," Clint answered. "I don't think anyone could talk Wes Hardin into doing something he didn't want to do. I talked to him, and then he left. The two may not be connected at all."

"I doubt that."

"We'll never know for sure because, hopefully, he'll never come back."

"Amen to that."

"I think I'll go and give Duke some exercise."

"Duke?" Neal Brown said.

"He's got this big black you have to see to believe," Wyatt Earp explained, his eyes lighting up.

"You mind if I come along?" Neal asked. "I feel like a ride myself."

"I'd welcome the company," Clint said.

"Keep your eyes open, Neal," Wyatt said, "and tell me everything you see."

"Gotcha, boss," Neal said, standing up.

"Let's go," Clint said, and both men left the marshal's office.

After they had left Ed Masterson said, "Do you really think that Clint talked Hardin into leaving?"

"I don't think it would have bothered Hardin's conscience any to gun down me or Tilghman—and he probably could have. The Gunsmith . . . that might have been another story, and maybe Hardin realized that."

"Is he that good?" Ed Masterson asked. "I mean, Bat says he is, but—"

"He's better than good," Wyatt said. "The Gunsmith is just about the best I've ever seen with a gun in his hand, and I've seen plenty."

"Why won't he wear a badge anymore?"

Wyatt removed his hat and scratched his head. "That's something personal with him. Maybe some day he'll let us all in on it."

Chapter Twenty-Seven

Clint and Neal Brown saddled up and rode north of town, coming to a stop on the rise where Clay Allison had camped the night before he rode into town.

"Wyatt was right about that horse," Neal said. "He's a beautiful animal."

"He's okay," Clint said, proudly patting Duke's neck. "We take good care of each other."

"I can understand that," Neal said. He stood up in his stirrups to look around and then asked, "When do you think those Texans will get here?"

"Who knows?" Clint replied. "Maybe never, if we get real lucky."

"I'd go for that," Neal said.

They rode farther north, then circled around and rode to the south.

"If they're coming from Texas, they'd come from the south," Neal Brown reasoned.

"Yeah," Clint said, "unless they circled around and

came in from the north to avoid being seen for as long as possible.''

"Why avoid being seen?'' Neal asked. "It's no secret that they're coming.''

"Who started the word spreading, I wonder?'' Clint said aloud, although the question was directed more at himself than at Neal. "I mean, if they're really on their way here to tear up the town, why advertise the fact? And why is it taking so long?''

"Maybe it's just a rumor,'' Neal Brown said with a shrug of his shoulders.

"What?''

"Maybe there are no Texans on their way,'' Neal said. "Maybe the whole thing is a gag.''

"A gag?'' Clint repeated. "You mean, all these precautions, all this manpower could be for nothing?''

"You think what?'' Wyatt Earp asked.

"Well, actually it was Neal who first brought it up,'' Clint explained, "but it's something we should consider, I think.''

"A joke?''

"A little more than a joke, maybe,'' Clint said. "A vicious lie, maybe, to get this whole town geared up for something that is never going to happen.''

Clint and Wyatt were alone in the marshal's office. Neal Brown had volunteered to return both horses to the stable while Clint went and talked to Marshal Earp.

"Who would do something like that?'' Wyatt asked. "Something so elaborate?''

"How elaborate is it to start a rumor? You know how rumors work, Wyatt,'' Clint said. "Very much the same as reputations do.''

"I know what you mean," Wyatt said. "But how do we verify such a thing?"

"Well, I haven't quite figured that out yet," Clint said. "Maybe you and your deputies—and the sheriff and his men—should get together and study on that."

"Not you?"

"I'm not a lawman, Wyatt, and it might be a good idea for me to stay away from Bill Tilghman for a while."

Wyatt studied Clint for a moment and then said, "Clint, I don't want you to take what I'm going to say wrong."

"Okay. What is it?"

"I'm glad to have your gun here, but you're free to leave if you want to. I think we've got enough firepower to handle almost any situation that may arise . . . and, if you're right, and there are no Texans on their way here, then you're just wasting your time."

"You want me to leave?" Clint said.

"I'm not asking or telling you to leave," Wyatt said. "I'm just giving you the opportunity."

"Bat is the one who asked me to come," Clint reminded the marshal.

"Talk to Bat, then. I'm sure he'd agree with me. We don't really need you here, Clint."

Clint frowned, because to him it sounded as if Wyatt were trying to get him out of town to protect him. Did the young marshal think that the Gunsmith was past his prime? And if so, why should that bother Clint, who had never liked being the Gunsmith, anyway?

For the first time in years he realized that there was a certain amount of pride attached to the reputation he had built up. A man had to be proud of what he was—to a certain degree—or else what was he on this earth for?

Clint Adams was certainly not there simply to mark time.

"You don't, huh?" he asked.

"We've got plenty of men, Clint," Wyatt said again.

"I see," Clint said.

As he started for the door Wyatt asked, "Where are you headed?"

"Over to the saloon," he said, not saying which one. "I think I'll get a drink and then sit my tired old bones down to a poker game."

"Clint, I didn't—" Wyatt started, wanting to explain his reasoning. He thought that perhaps Clint had indeed taken his words the wrong way.

"If you see Bat, tell him I'm around, will you?" Clint asked.

"Sure, Clint."

The Gunsmith left, mildly shocked at himself as he found himself hoping that they were not dealing with a rumor after all.

Chapter Twenty-Eight

Clint had chosen the Alamo saloon at random and, true to his word, grabbed a beer and found a card game. Seated with a comfortable view of the front entrance, he proceeded to play some serious poker. The other players at the table were unfortunate enough to be the recipient of the Gunsmith's anger and confusion in response to Wyatt Earp's words. He was confused because he could not quite figure out why he was angry at being told he wasn't needed. Consequently, he sought to immerse himself in the game of poker, and almost immediately began raking in a tidy profit.

Wyatt Earp had found Bat Masterson following his conversation with Clint Adams, and had relayed Clint and Neal Brown's thoughts on the possibility that they were all responding to nothing more than a rumor.

"It's an interesting idea," Bat said, "and, as a matter of fact, one that I prefer."

"So do I, but what can we do to check it out?"

"We'd need somebody who has a few friends in Texas," Bat said. "Who fits that bill better than Clint?"

"Clint?"

"From what I can see, he's more or less been based in Texas these past few years. Seems to hole up there whenever he's not traveling."

"Bat, I haven't seen Clint since Deadman's flats, but I understand you have."

"Once, but I haven't seen him in a while."

"Has he changed, or is it me?"

"He's changed, all right," Bat said. "I've already commented on that. He's bitter."

"I've noticed that, but why?"

"He's been carrying a rep around with him for a long time, Wyatt, and an unwanted rep at that. He never wanted to be *the Gunsmith*. All he ever wanted to be was a good lawman. When he lost that, he started to change."

"But he didn't lose it, he gave it up," Wyatt pointed out.

"I guess he feels he was forced to give it up."

"You know, I first met him and Bill Hickok not long after he'd given up his badge. He was confused then. When we met again in Caldwell, Kansas he seemed content, but now he's a totally different man."

"What can I say?" Bat replied. "Who knows what we'll be like in ten or fifteen years?"

"He reacted funny a little while ago, when we talked," Wyatt said.

"How so?"

Wyatt related the conversation, and the Gunsmith's reaction to being told that he wasn't needed.

"Obviously, he took it wrong," Bat said. "He may

have thought that you were trying to get him out of the way.''

"Get him out of the way?'' Wyatt said. "Why would he think that? None of us can match him with a gun. If it comes to a fight, I'd want him on my side, but we're all wearing badges, Bat. This is our job.''

"He must feel an obligation to me, then,'' Bat reasoned. "I had no idea that the help that was coming was going to be you and my brother. I thought we might need help, and I contacted him and asked him to come.''

"Is he getting sensitive in his old age, or what?''

"That may be it, even though you're joking about it,'' Bat said. "He's over forty, you know.''

"That's not so old,'' Wyatt said.

"It might feel old when the rest of the people around you are under thirty, like you, me, Ed, Tilghman, and probably even Neal.''

"I guess. I just never thought Clint would react this way to getting older.''

"See?'' Bat said. "You've got it too.''

"What?''

"This thing about his rep. I'm not criticizing you. I find myself doing the same thing. I did it with Hickok, and I do it with Clint.''

"Do what?''

"Forget that behind *the Gunsmith*, and behind *Wild Bill*, there's a man. Hickok proved to all of us that he was human when he got killed. Maybe this is Clint's way of proving that he's human.''

"I guess a rep can do that to you, huh?'' Wyatt said, thinking about his own growing reputation. Although Wyatt was only twenty-eight, already stories were circulating through the West about his exploits in the Kansas towns of Ellsworth and Wichita. There was even a story of how Wyatt had embarrassed and defeated the legendary Ben Thompson in a gunfight, which was total fiction.

"There's one thing I know for sure about Clint," Bat said.

"What's that?"

"He's the best man I've ever seen with a gun, bar none," Bat said. "Even better than Ben Thompson."

"You never saw Hickok, did you?" Wyatt asked.

"Never had the pleasure. Was he better than Clint?"

Shaking his head Wyatt said, "They were damned close, I'll tell you that. The three of us had it out with six men in a Texas saloon when I first met them,"* Wyatt went on, "and I know their two hit the floor before mine did, but who was faster? They didn't even know, and neither of them cared to find out. They were too close as friends for that."

Bat's own remark about Ben Thompson had reminded him of the stories he had heard, and he asked Wyatt about them.

"No truth in it at all," Wyatt said. "I met Ben in Ellsworth, but we never squared off."

"Interesting how stories get started, isn't it?" Bat asked.

"Yeah," Wyatt said. "Stories, rumors, reputations . . ."

"I think I'll go and find Clint," Bat said.

"I'll take a walk."

Both men stood up and left the marshal's office, and as they got to the boardwalk outside Bat saw a man riding down Front Street.

*The Gunsmith #1: Macklin's Women

"Well, well," he said. "Speak of the devil and up he pops. No sooner do we get rid of Wes Hardin . . ."

"What are you talking about?" Wyatt asked.

"We've got us another distinguished visitor," he said, pointing towards the rider, and when Wyatt turned and looked he knew what Bat meant.

The man on the horse was Ben Thompson.

Ben Thompson was not quite the concern that John Wesley Hardin had been. Hardin was a killer while Thompson, although he was a known gunman, did not have a reputation as an arbitrary killer. Still, Thompson would have to be watched while he was in Dodge, and it helped that both Bat and Wyatt had met the gunman before.

Thompson apparently had not seen either lawman as he rode by the marshal's office, and neither man felt inclined to step out into the street to attract his attention just yet.

"Clint knows Ben, doesn't he?" Wyatt asked.

"Better than we do, I think."

"Maybe we had both better go and talk to him," the marshal suggested.

"Good idea," Bat agreed. "Clint might be able to question Ben about what he's doing in Dodge without getting him upset."

"Just what I was thinking," Wyatt said. "Come on."

It looked as if the Gunsmith was needed in Dodge after all.

Chapter Twenty-Nine

The two lawmen had checked the Alhambra and Long Branch saloons first before finally locating the Gunsmith in the Alamo, where he had amassed an impressive pile of cash in front of him. Noticing that Clint's beer mug was nearly empty, Bat went to the bar for a fresh one to replace it, and then both men approached the table.

"Seem to be doing pretty well for yourself," Bat commented, placing the mug next to him.

Clint looked up, saw his two friends and smiled. He was in a good humor now, brought about by an incredible run of luck with the cards.

"Sit down, boys, and I'll take some of your money too," Clint said. The nearly empty mug of beer was actually still his first, for the Gunsmith drank very lightly, if at all, while playing poker.

"Think you could call it quits for a while?" Wyatt asked. "I'd like to talk to you."

Clint cast a regretful look at the faces of the other

players, and said, "Looks like the law caught up to me, fellas. Keep my seat warm, will you?"

"Sure," one of the players said as he watched Clint pick up his winnings.

As Clint walked to a rear table with Bat and Wyatt a man at the table grumbled, "Maybe now that he's gone somebody else can win a pot."

"Shut up and deal," another man said, and the game went on.

At the back table, while Clint stuffed his winnings into his pockets, Bat said, "Ben Thompson just rode into town."

"Ben?"

"You know him pretty well, don't you?" Wyatt asked.

"As well as anyone, I guess," Clint said. "I haven't seen him in a few years, though. What about you? I heard something about you and him—"

"We met, but never crossed swords," Wyatt said.

Clint nodded knowingly. "I figured it was something like that. Well, Ben won't be the problem Hardin might have been. He avoids trouble whenever he can, and would rather gamble than use his gun."

"I know that," Wyatt said, "but I'd still like to know what he's doing in Dodge."

"And you want me to find out?"

"I don't think he'd respond well to a man with a badge asking him," Wyatt said. "So, yes, I'm asking for your help."

Clint finished stuffing his money away and sipped on the new beer supplied by Bat.

"All right," he said finally. "No problem. It'd be natural for Ben and me to talk, since we haven't seen each other in a while."

"Are you friends?" Wyatt asked.

"I wouldn't go that far," Clint said. "I was in Abilene when he and his family were injured. He and Phil Coe were partners then, but Ben wasn't part of the finale, there. He had gotten hurt earlier and was laid up by the time matters came to a head. I worked as a dealer for him briefly in Newton, Kansas, just before we met up in Caldwell. Friends? I wouldn't say that, but it wouldn't be unusual for us to have a drink together."

"Good. He's probably registering at a hotel now."

"Well, I doubt he'll go to the Alamo for a drink," Clint said, "since that was the name of the saloon that Thompson and Coe's saloon had been in competition with in Abilene. I guess we'll just have to wait and see which place he picks for his drinking and gambling, and I'll approach him there."

"Thanks, Clint," Wyatt said. "I appreciate this. Uh, listen, about before—"

"Forget before, Wyatt," Clint said. "I'm just getting sensitive in my old age."

"That's what I said," Wyatt blurted before he could stop himself.

Clint noticed the sheepish look on his friend's face and said, "Well, you were right."

Wyatt grinned and then said to Bat, "We'd better get to work."

"There was something else," Bat reminded him.

"Oh, yeah," Wyatt said. "Clint, do you think you could send out some telegrams to some friends in Texas?"

"About this rumor business?" Clint asked.

"Right."

"I could send a couple, I guess, but there's no guarantee that anybody will know anything."

"Well, they'd have a better chance of hearing than we would," Wyatt said.

"You might be right," Clint agreed. "I'll give it a try."

"Good," Wyatt said.

Both lawmen stood up and Bat said, "Stay away from that poker, Clint. I don't think you made any friends there."

"I don't play friends to make poker, if you know what I mean," Clint said, smiling.

"You better not have any more beer, either," Bat said, and he and Wyatt left.

Clint remained where he was finishing his beer, having no desire to return to the poker table. There was no point in pushing his luck.

Wes Hardin, he thought, *and now Ben Thompson . . .*

More and more like Abilene . . .

Chapter Thirty

When the dust had settled, Ben Thompson had headed for the Long Branch Saloon. Later that same day Clint walked into the Long Branch and saw Thompson working a table, and knew that he didn't have to ask Thompson why he had come to Dodge, since it was obvious that he was working there as a house dealer. Still, the natural thing was to approach the man and talk to him.

Thompson was dealing faro, which was not one of the Gunsmith's favorite games. Clint went to the bar to get a beer, then walked over to the table and watched while Thompson dealt a hand. He did not speak until the hand was over.

"Hello, Ben."

Thompson looked up with an expressionless face, but when he saw Clint his "dealer's" face dropped away and was replaced by something less than overwhelming pleasure. It was possible that seeing Clint had brought back the pain of Abilene.

"Clint Adams," he said. "What are you doing here?"

"I've been here for a week or so," Clint said. "I was about to ask you the same thing."

Thompson indicated the table and said, "I'm working."

"Got time for a drink?"

Thompson hesitated, then said, "Yes, I suppose I do. Let me get a relief dealer."

Clint waited a few moments, and when Thompson was free they moved to an empty table, both men sitting so that they could see the entire room. Clint wondered what would have happened if he, Hickok, Thompson and Wes Hardin had all ever tried to sit at the same round table.

Thompson signaled the bartender for a beer, and when he had it asked Clint, "What brought you to Dodge?"

"Bat Masterson is a deputy here," Clint said, "and Wyatt Earp the marshal. Both are friends of mine."

Thompson frowned. "I knew Bat was here. When did Wyatt Earp get appointed marshal?"

"Very recently," Clint said. "You should probably know that there's a rumor of trouble brewing."

"The thing about the Texans?"

"You know about that?"

"I suspect it's one of the reasons that Chalk Beeson offered me a job here," Thompson said, "but if he thinks he's hiring my gun by hiring me as a dealer, he's sadly mistaken. I appreciate the fact that you mentioned it, though."

"Sure. It's something I'd want to know if I was in your shoes."

"You're not wearing a badge?" Thompson asked.

Clint shook his head and said, "Not since Abilene," although that wasn't strictly true. He had worn a badge once since Abilene, but that had been a special case.

"You?" he asked.

"Me? No, not for a long time," Thompson said. "Gambling's my game, not the law."

"You know both Bat and Wyatt, don't you?"

"Bat better than Wyatt," Thompson said.

"I've heard rumors about you and Wyatt in Ellsworth, but he tells me it's a lot of hogwash."

"Glad to hear he's telling it right," Thompson said. "He's an honorable man. He could have ridden that rumor for all it was worth."

"Not Wyatt."

"I realize that . . . now," Thompson said, sounding as if he'd had his doubts in the past. Thompson was deadly with a gun, and Clint would not hold out much hope for Wyatt Earp if Thompson took it in his mind to go after him. Aside from Hickok, Thompson was the best man with a gun that Clint had ever seen. He had no idea how he himself would fair against Ben Thompson, and he had no desire to find out.

"Are you planning to stay in town much longer?" Thompson asked.

"I may stick around to see if this rumored trouble comes to pass," Clint said. "How about you?"

"Just looking to build up a poke before I move on," Thompson said. "Tell Earp I'm not here to stir up trouble."

"If he asks, I'll tell him."

Thompson gave Clint a long look, then said, "Sure. If he asks you can tell him."

Thompson finished his beer and then said, "Well, I better get back to work. Doesn't look good for me to be goofing off on the first day."

"No, I guess not," Clint agreed.

"It was nice seeing you, Clint," Thompson said politely, rising.

"I'll see you around town," Clint replied.

"Come and play my table."

Shaking his head Clint said, "Faro's not my game. I'll stick to poker."

"Suit yourself," Thompson said, and returned to work. Clint stayed only long enough to finish his beer, and then left the Long Branch, satisfied that Ben Thompson was not a threat to the "tranquility" of Dodge City.

Not intentionally, anyway.

Clint went looking for Earp or Bat and found Wyatt in his office with Ed Masterson.

"I talked to Thompson a few minutes ago," Clint said.

"What did you find out?" Wyatt asked, and Ed Masterson leaned forward with interest.

"Apparently Chalk Beeson sent for him to be a dealer in the Long Branch," Clint said. "Thompson himself hasn't ruled out the possibility that Beeson might think he was hiring his gun at the same time."

"And?"

"And Thompson says no way. He's being paid to deal, and that's all he intends to do."

"Did you tell him about the trouble?" Ed asked.

"He knew about it already," Clint said. "That's why he thinks Beeson might be depending on his gun."

"Why'd he come, Clint?"

"He's got to work to build up a poke," Clint said, shrugging. "This is as good a place as any, I guess. He knew Bat was here, but he didn't know you were, Wyatt."

"How did he react?"

"It didn't mean much to him," Clint said. "The fact that you were telling the truth about Ellsworth did, though. He says you're an honorable man."

"I appreciate that," Wyatt said. "I'd rather have him thinking that than coming after me."

"I don't blame you."

"What about those telegrams?"

"I've still got that to do," Clint answered, "as soon as I decide who to send them to. Who are you going to have watching Thompson?"

"Probably Neal," Wyatt said. "He knows me and Bat, and he'd probably pick Ed out as Bat's brother. Why?"

"He gave me a message for you," Clint said, "if you happened to ask, that is."

"What's the message?"

"That he's in Dodge to deal faro, not to start trouble."

"That's comforting," Wyatt said.

"Of course," Clint went on, "speaking from personal experience I know that you don't have to be looking for trouble to find it . . . or cause it."

Chapter Thirty-One

It didn't take long for trouble to find Ben Thompson. Clint was having dinner at the Dodge House with Bat and Ed Masterson when someone rushed in and yelled out, "Trouble at the Long Branch." The words were no sooner out of his mouth than there were two shots which could very well have come from the saloon, since it was just down the street.

"Neal must be there," Ed said, but he and his brother rose just the same, and Clint followed.

There was a small crowd of people in front of the Long Branch, some of whom had been outside and were trying to look in, and others who had been inside and were trying to get out.

"Make way!" Ed Masterson shouted as he and Bat fought their way through the crowd. Clint played it the easy way and followed in their wake.

When they got inside they found that the place had more than half emptied out, and they looked around for where the trouble had originated. Since Clint had already seen what table Thompson was working, he looked there and saw the man slumped over the table. Ben Thompson was still behind the table, and his hands were empty. Neal Brown had one hand on the slumped over man, apparently checking to see if there was any sign of life.

"There," Clint said, indicating Thompson's table.

"Neal!" Ed called out.

As the three men advanced on the scene Neal Brown turned and said, "He's dead."

"Who is he?"

Thompson answered before Neal Brown could.

"Fella I had some trouble with a little while back," he explained. "It was just a coincidence that he happened to walk in here tonight. I guess he still held a grudge."

"Neal?" Bat said, asking for Brown's eyewitness account of what had happened, but before the deputy marshal could speak Wyatt Earp entered the saloon and joined them.

"What's the story here, Neal?" he asked, and Brown went on with his explanation.

"Self-defense, Marshal, pure and simple," he said. "This fella," he said, indicating the dead man, "just walked up to Thompson's table, shouted something at him and went for his gun. Thompson was faster."

"Where were you?" Wyatt asked.

"I was standing at the bar," Brown answered. "I saw the man walk up to the table, but I had no way of knowing what he was going to do. It happened so fast, Marshal, that I barely had a chance to move before it was over."

"Don't blame your deputy, Marshal," Thompson spoke up. "He acted as fast as any man could have, but it was over in the blink of an eye. This fella just had a death wish, is all."

Wyatt stepped forward to examine the dead man briefly, then he said, "Neal, grab some of those rubber-neckers outside and have them take the body out."

"Right, Marshal."

Conversation was suspended while two men removed the body from the saloon, and then Wyatt faced Thompson across the table with his arms folded across his chest.

"You can have my gun if you like, Wyatt," Thompson said.

"Ben, you're lucky that one of my deputies was here to witness the whole thing, or I'd have you and your gun in my jail, right now."

"Right fortunate, Marshal," Thompson agreed.

"I guess there's nothing I can do about a man's past catching up to him in my town," Wyatt Earp went on, "but I know you'll try to avoid any further trouble from here on in."

"Marshal, I'm a peaceable man," Ben Thompson explained. "I always try to avoid trouble."

"I'll count on that, Ben," Wyatt said.

Chalk Beeson stepped forward at that point and said, "Marshal, can I start my business up again?"

"Who are you?" He hadn't been in town long enough to meet everyone.

"This is Chalk Beeson, Wyatt," Bat said, stepping forward. "He owns the Long Branch."

"Along with my partner, Bill Harris," Beeson added. "I'd like to bring the people back in, if that's all right, Marshal."

"It's all right with me, Mr. Beeson," Wyatt said, "but you better do something about this table."

"What's the matter with it?"

"I don't know about anyone else," Wyatt said, "but I wouldn't take kindly to having to gamble my money at a table with fresh blood on it."

Beeson looked down at the felt top of the table and saw the fresh puddle of blood soaking into it.

"Jesus!" he said in disgust, throwing Thompson a look, as if it was his fault that the man had fallen forward instead of back.

"In the future," Thompson said to Beeson, "I'll try and use a larger caliber gun."

Clint guessed that Thompson was wearing his Colt Cloverleaf beneath his right arm. If he'd been wearing a .45, the man would have been thrown halfway across the room.

"Jesus!" Beeson said again.

Chapter Thirty-Two

By the next morning Clint had decided who to send his telegrams to in Texas. Despite what Wyatt Earp and Bat Masterson might have thought, the Gunsmith did not have all that many friends in the state of Texas. Even he found it odd that, with all his traveling, he always found himself gravitating back to Texas.

He had breakfast with Bat, who asked him about the telegrams, and he told him that he was going to send a couple out right after breakfast.

"Only a couple?"

"There aren't that many people in Texas that I would trust to give me the straight information, Bat," Clint explained. "These two should do the trick though. If there's anything to be found out, they'll find it out."

"Okay," Bat said. "I hope we can resolve this one way or the other. The suspense is killing me."

"What's the matter," Clint said, "don't you like surprises?"

"Only in my bed."

"The only surprise there is when someone else is in there with you," Clint said, teasing his young friend.

"Ha!" Bat replied, and began talking about his countless conquests among the opposite sex.

After breakfast Bat walked to the telegraph office with Clint and watched while Clint wrote out one message and had it sent to two different people in two different Texas towns.

Clint sent one telegram to a man named Rich Hartman in Labyrinth, Texas.

The second message went to the Kennedy Ranch, near Lansdale, Texas.

"They have their own telegraph office?" Bat asked when he heard that.

"Oh, yes," Clint said. "The Kennedy spread is the largest in that area of Texas."

Clint had been involved in a "wet stock" battle between the Kennedy spread and a spread across the river, in Mexico. He had done both spreads a good turn by exposing the culprits and stopping a war.

After the telegrams were sent Clint said, "I guess we've got Texas pretty well covered with just those two telegrams. With any luck, Hartman and Kennedy will send out some telegrams of their own, and we'll know soon enough whether or not we're really going to get a visit from a pack of irate Texans."

"Can't be soon enough for me," Bat said. "I'll go over and tell Wyatt that you've sent the telegrams."

"Fine," Clint said.

"What are you going to do?"

"I don't know," Clint replied. It was too early for a poker game, too early for a drink. "I think I'll go up to my room and clean my guns."

"Hey, good idea," Bat said. "You want to do mine too?"

"What next?" Clint said. "Are you going to ask me to do your laundry?"

"Let me know as soon as you get an answer," Bat said.

"Be patient, Bat," Clint said. "If my people send out telegrams of their own, we won't get an answer for a while. Learn patience, my young friend."

"Okay, Pop. See you later."

Clint went back to the Dodge House and up to his room, where he grabbed his Springfield, took his tools out of his saddlebags and started working on the rifle first. He was just about to start on his modified Colt when there was a knock on the door.

He put the rifle aside and went to open the door.

"Oh, hello, Maggie," he said.

"Hello, Clint. Can I come in?"

"Uh, sure, come in," he said. He felt uncomfortable with her, but what had she expected from him after they spent one night together? He had thought that she was old enough to realize that a relationship did not develop after one lone night.

"I'm a little disappointed that we haven't . . . seen each other since . . . that night," she said, and then she hurriedly added, "Although I understand that nothing was said about anything . . . between us."

"I've been, uh, very busy," Clint said, lamely. He had no way of knowing if Maggie knew anything about Amy Vining, and didn't want to mention it himself.

"I realize that," she said, "and I also realize that you might have . . . seen someone else while you've been here."

"Uh—"

"Don't say anything, Clint," she said. "I don't really know why I came up here. I guess I just wanted you to know that I don't really expect anything from you."

"I see."

There was an awkward silence then, and it was broken by Maggie, whose tone suddenly changed.

"Oh, hell," she said. "I guess I really came up here to see if you would want to make love to me."

"Oh?"

"Do you still find me desirable?" she asked. "Or was that just a first night in town thing?"

"No, of course not," Clint said, taking her by the shoulders. "You're a very desirable woman, Maggie."

"Then make love to me," she said, backing away from him. "Make love to me now and I won't bother you anymore."

"You're not bothering me, Maggie—" he started to say, but his words caught in his throat as she hurriedly began to undress. When her full, pale breasts bobbed into view he could see that her nipples were already hard, and when she was totally naked the sharp, tangy scent of her arousal drifted up to his nostrils. It was an exciting smell, and in her earthy way, Maggie Lane was an exciting woman.

As she came to him he palmed her breasts, feeling the nipples scrape his palms, and captured her mouth with his. Her hands snaked between them and began to eagerly undo his pants, and when she fished out his hard, pulsating member, she fell to her knees and popped it into her mouth and began working on it avidly.

To say the least, this was better than cleaning his guns!

Chapter Thirty-Three

Clint was always amazed at how quickly the time passed while he was playing poker.

In that respect, poker had a lot in common with sex. So after Maggie left and he'd finished working on his guns, he tried his hand at a table at the Alhambra this time. These were totally different players, but his luck was still holding. Had he not already had a reason to stay in Dodge City, he might have stayed just to ride out this streak of luck.

He had been playing for hours when Bat Masterson entered the saloon with the telegraph clerk trailing behind him.

"Clint," Bat said, approaching the table.

Clint looked up first at Bat, and then at the clerk, and realized immediately what had happened.

He had gotten an answer.

"Gentlemen," he said, picking up his winnings, "thanks very much for the game."

138

There were some grumblings about him leaving while he was ahead, but no one dared say anything aloud to him because they were all aware of who he was.

"Over here," Clint said, and they moved to a table in the rear of the room.

"All right," he said to the clerk, "let me have it."

The clerk passed over the message, and Clint tipped him and let him leave before reading it.

"What's it say?" Bat asked.

"I think we had better show this to Wyatt," Clint said.

"What's it say?" Bat repeated.

"It looks like we're going to have company after all," Clint said, handing his friend the telegram.

It was from the Kennedy Ranch near Lansdale, Texas, and very briefly it said that the rumor he had been asking about had been confirmed.

"They're on their way," Clint said.

Chapter Thirty-Four

While Wyatt Earp was reading the telegram, the clerk entered the marshal's office and handed Clint a second message. This one was from Rick Hartman, in Labyrinth, Texas, and carried much the same message.

After Wyatt read the second one he said, "Well, it looks like there's no doubt about it, gentlemen. We might have a problem on our hands very soon."

"Any indication as to when they'll be here?" Neal Brown asked.

Wyatt scanned both messages, then shook his head and said, "No, and there's no indication about how many, either."

"If we don't know how many, how can we get set up for them?" Neal wanted to know.

Wyatt shrugged, but Clint said, "Cover the saloons."

"What?" Wyatt asked.

"We cover the saloons," Clint said. "I mean, where does most of Dodge City's revenue come from?"

"The gambling in the saloons," Bat Masterson said.

"Right. These fellas aren't just going to ride into town and start busting the place up. They'll ride in, get settled a bit maybe, and then they'll head for a saloon."

"Which one?" Neal asked.

"They'll split up, so many in say, the three or four biggest houses in town."

"They'll gamble for a while," Bat said.

"And then they'll start a ruckus," Wyatt added.

"And during the ruckus they'll bust up the saloons."

Wyatt looked at Bat and asked, "What do you think?"

"We've got to do something," Bat said. "That sounds like as good a plan as any."

"What plan?" Neal asked, looking confused.

"We'll have to split up," Wyatt said, "and cover—how many of us are there?"

"Seven," Bat supplied.

"Okay, seven," Wyatt said. "We'll have to split up and cover maybe three of the saloons."

"Which ones?" Neal asked.

Up to this point, Bill Tilghman had remained quiet, but he chose to answer that question.

"The Long Branch, the Alhambra, and the Alamo," he said. "They're the three biggest."

"Okay," Wyatt said. "That's the way we'll do it. Agreed?"

Clint, Bat and Tilghman agreed. Ed Masterson was over at the Long Branch keeping an eye on Thompson, but Bat knew he would agree, as well. It was Neal Brown who still looked confused.

"So when this big group of men rides into town, we hightail it to the saloons—"

"I don't think they'll all come in at once," Clint said.

"And maybe not even on the same day," Tilghman said.

"You both have a point," Wyatt said.

"We'll have to be on the lookout and pick them out as they come into town," Bat said.

"How do we do that?" Neal asked.

"We'll just have to hope we get lucky," Wyatt said. "Some Texans can't help but look like Texans."

"We can tell some of them from the brands on their animals," Tilghman suggested.

"Good idea, Bill," Wyatt said.

"What happens if they do all come in at once?" Neal Brown asked.

"What are you, the devil's advocate?" Bat asked.

"Huh?"

"Forget it," Clint said. "We'll just have to be prepared for that too, Neal, if it happens that way, but I don't think it will."

"I'll have to talk to Bassett about this," Wyatt said.

"I'll go with you," Tilghman volunteered.

"All right, Bill. Bat, maybe you'd better go over and talk to Ed, make sure he knows what's happening."

"Right."

"In fact, bring him back here, and I'll bring Bassett back," Wyatt said. "We can go over our plans tonight and make sure we all know what our part is."

"Good idea," Clint said.

"Uh, Clint," Wyatt said, "what about Thompson?"

"You want me to ask him to help?"

"It's worth a try," Wyatt said. "His gun would be a big addition to our force."

Clint scratched his chin as he thought it over, then said, "Well, I can give it a try."

"Okay. Let's go. We'll meet back here as soon as we can," Wyatt said, standing up.

Neal Brown was the only one who did not have something to do, and he remained seated where he was, but as they were leaving they heard him say, "Seven, maybe eight of us against how many Texans?"

Bat turned around and said, "The poor bastards."

"Who?" Neal asked.

"The Texans."

Neal's frown deepened and he asked, "Why?"

Bat grinned and said, "They're outnumbered before they even get here."

Chapter Thirty-Five

Clint and Bat went over to the Long Branch, and while Bat talked to his brother at the bar, Clint walked over to Ben Thompson's faro table.

"I'd like to talk to you for a couple of minutes, Ben," Clint said.

"Shall I get a relief dealer?"

"That's not necessary," Clint said. "We've confirmed the rumor about the Texans that are heading this way."

"I see."

"We're gearing up to handle them when they get here."

"You putting on a badge?"

"No, but I'm lending a hand."

"Mmm-hmm," Ben said, dealing out another hand to his customers. "And what do you want from me?"

"Marshal Earp wanted me to ask you if you'd be willing to stand with us," Clint said.

"He did, huh?"

"Yes."

"This isn't your idea, huh?"

"No."

Ben Thompson nodded and raked in his chips. "Well, apologize to the marshal for me, will you, Clint?" Thompson asked. "Tell him I'm a dealer these days."

"All right."

"Still—" Thompson added, stopping short.

"Yeah?"

Now Thompson looked directly at the Gunsmith so that there would not be any misunderstanding. "If those Texans should happen to come in here and try to disrupt my table . . ." Thompson said, and he let it trail off, allowing his eyes to finish the sentence for him.

"I understand, Ben," Clint said.

"Good," Thompson said, and went back to his game.

Clint walked to the bar where Bat and Ed were standing, watching him.

"What's the story?" Bat asked.

"He's a dealer, not a deputy," Clint said.

"That's too bad," Ed said.

"Not really," Clint said.

"Why?" Bat asked.

"Let's go talk to Wyatt."

The three of them left the Long Branch and walked back to the marshal's office. When they arrived Wyatt was already there with Charlie Bassett.

"Did you talk to Thompson?" he asked Clint.

"I did," Clint answered. "He won't commit himself to helping us—"

"Shit!"

"—but if the fracas should happen to work its way into the Long Branch and threaten his game . . ."

Wyatt gave in to a tight grin and said, "I see. All right, then, let's make our plans. Sheriff, are you with us?"

"Cooperation, right?" Bassett said. "I'm with you, and so are my deputies."

"Good," Wyatt said. He looked seriously at Clint and said, "Clint, you want to pin a badge on for this?"

"I'd rather not."

"Suit yourself."

"I usually do."

The plans were made for the seven lawmen to split up the three saloons—Alamo, Alhambra and Long Branch—among them. Bat and Ed would cover the Alamo; Wyatt, Neal Brown and Charlie Bassett would handle the Alhambra; and Clint and Bill Tilghman would take the Long Branch. In fact, Clint was sending a message to Wyatt with his eyes, hoping that his friend would be able to read it and assign Tilghman to go with him.

Also, Wyatt's original plan was for three of them to cover the Long Branch, while the other saloons were handled by two men each, but Clint pointed out that Ben Thompson was in the Long Branch already and that Thompson would not stand by and watch them get shot, if it came to that.

"All right," Wyatt agreed and the Alhambra, being the second largest, was assigned three men.

Wyatt announced that there would always be one man on either side of Front Street, watching for strangers riding into town. The chances were good that the Texans would ride in two, three or four at a time, but not alone, and not in large, unwieldy groups. It always seemed that a lone man or a large group attracted more attention than a few friends riding into town together.

"As soon as you think you've got some of them spotted," Wyatt said, "one of you peel off and inform the rest of us."

"We'll have to keep count," Clint said. "We don't know how many are going to come, but I would say that it would have to be between twelve and twenty. As soon as we've counted them up somewhere in between there, we'll have to start covering the saloons."

"I think one of us should be in the saloons anyway," Wyatt said. "I'm going to leave it up to you boys to break up the time covering the street and the saloons."

"What will you be doing?" Bassett asked.

"I think I'm going to talk to the mayor and the townspeople and see if I can't get us some volunteer deputies."

"Fat chance," Bassett said. "We got mostly gamblers, drunks and drifters in Dodge, and you ain't gonna find many volunteers among that crowd."

"Still, I better give it a try," Wyatt said. "Clint's estimate of twelve to twenty just may turn out to be conservative."

"Huh?" Bassett said.

"He means it could also turn out to be thirty or forty," Bill Tilghman said.

"Jesus," Bassett said, shaking his head.

"Those are mighty steep odds," Neal Brown said.

"We've faced steep odds before," Bat pointed out. Basically he was referring to him and his brother, and Wyatt and Clint, but no one disputed his statement.

"Ed, why don't you and the boys start divvying up the shifts," Wyatt said, "and I'll go talk to Mayor Hoover."

"Right, Wyatt."

Before leaving Wyatt looked at Clint and said, "I'm glad you didn't take me at my word the other day."

"When have I ever taken you at your word, Marshal?"
Clint asked.

"I think I've just been insulted," Wyatt said, "but
we'll talk about it another time."

Wyatt left and Ed Masterson stood up as they began
discussing shifts.

They agreed to cover the street in three eight-hour
shifts, working it out so that while two men were on the
street the others would be split among the three saloons.
After the saloons closed, two men would cover the street
into the night while the others slept. There was always a
chance that some of the Texans might try to slip into town
at night, and they didn't want any surprises if that should
happen.

Once they had their plan set up, they put it into effect
immediately, with Ed Masterson and Bill Tilghman taking the street right then and there, and the others heading
for the saloons, with the exception of Charlie Bassett, who
went back to his office. Bat headed for the Alamo, Neal
Brown went and took up position in the Alhambra, and
Clint went to the Long Branch to kill the time the best way
he knew how, in a poker game.

He had to stay in the saloon anyway, right?

Chapter Thirty-Six

The first four rode in the next morning, while Clint and Bat were covering the street. Clint saw them first and sank back into the shadows in front of the sheriff's office. Bat was only a few seconds behind him, and likewise sank into a doorway as the four men rode by on their way to the livery.

Clint recognized the brand on two of the horses as coming from Texas outfits, which didn't have to mean that the men also came from there, but they had to use some kind of an identifying system, and the brands were as good as any. They would rather pad their count than be surprised by more when the crunch came.

As prearranged, Bat left his post and went to inform the others that the first four had arrived. He would then return to the street as one of the other deputies discreetly checked to see where the four men would find accommodations.

The night before Wyatt had broken the not surprising news that there would be no volunteer deputies. Clint had gone through the same thing recently while in Lancaster, Texas.* The townspeople elected officials to fight for them, and resented it when they were asked to help themselves.

That's what they paid lawmen for, wasn't it?

Sure.

During the rest of that day, five more men arrived, first by two, and then three, and all during Ed Masterson and Bill Tilghman's afternoon shift.

By nightfall they were pretty sure that they had nine Texans staying in town, having taken rooms in three different hotels. The men were also drinking or gambling in three different saloons.

The Alamo, the Alhambra, and the Long Branch.

So far, things were going as expected.

*The Gunsmith #18: High Noon at Lancaster

Chapter Thirty-Seven

That night, Amy Vining came to Clint in his room.

"It's been so long," she murmured against his mouth.

"Yes," he agreed.

They undressed and he carried her to the bed, where he devoted an extended amount of time to exploring her full, young body with his mouth and tongue.

"Oh, yes, Clint," she said when he had thrust his tongue deep inside of her. He flicked his tongue around, in and out, and then moved up and fastened his lips on her stiff little bud. He sucked on it and bit until she drove her hips up into his face, gasping as the force of her orgasm overcame her.

"Oh, God," she said when he released her and moved up to lie next to her.

"You're so hard," she said, touching his rigid member. "So hard and so hot."

She rolled on top of him and began kissing his chest and sucking and nipping at his nipples. He cupped the firm cheeks of her ass while she kissed his shoulder, neck and face, and then he had to let go as she slid her tongue down his body until she was running up and down his throbbing shaft. She made an "Mmmm" sound as she opened her mouth and took him inside, and then he cupped the back of her head in his hands as her head began to bob up and down at increasing speed until a river of semen shot from him into her mouth and she took it all in.

A little later she asked, "The trouble in this town is coming to a head, isn't it, Clint?"

"Yes," he said. "Very soon."

"And when it's all over you'll leave?"

"Yes," he said, deciding to be very honest. "You never expected that I would stay, did you, Amy?"

"No," she said, laying her head on his chest. "I've thought about it, hoped for it, even prayed for it a little, but no, I never really expected it."

"Good," he said. "Then you won't be that disappointed."

"Oh, I'll be disappointed," she assured him. "Don't worry about that."

"Not for long, though," he said. "You'll find some nice young man and settle down."

"Probably," she said, "but I don't want to talk about that now."

She reached for his limp penis and began to knead it gently, enjoying the feel of it as it grew in her hands.

"I'm wet," she said, easing atop him. She guided the head of his swollen penis to her damp portal and he slid in so easily, going all the way down to the root.

She sat up on him and he reached up to tweak her nipples while she rode him. Her head was thrown back as she ground herself against him, tangling her fine pubic hair with his coarse, wiry black ones.

When he felt her trembling and ready to come, he lifted his hips, raising them both up, and then released himself so that they came together.

"You've got to go," he told her later.

"Why?"

"Because I need my rest."

"I won't bother you."

"I might get called away during the night," he said. "It wouldn't do for you to be found here. Go home, Amy."

"All right," she said, glumly.

He watched her as she dressed and then wordlessly walked to the door with her shoulders slumped.

"Good night," he said.

"Be careful," she said.

"Sure," he answered. *But that wasn't part of the plan,* he was thinking.

Chapter Thirty-Eight

Over breakfast Bat said, "Two more came in during the night."

"Together?"

"Separately. I guess they figured it would be easier to sneak in one at a time."

"That makes eleven," Clint said. "Who spotted them?"

"Ed. He left Neal on the street and went to watch the livery. They got past Neal, but not Ed."

"Good."

"How many do you figure on, Clint?"

"I don't know," he said, "but after the next bunch we better be ready for action. Three or four more ride in and they'll have enough to cause plenty of trouble."

"More than enough."

"Have you recognized any of them?" Clint asked.

"No, why?"

"You haven't seen this fella Texas Bill, huh?"

"Unless he came in during the night," Bat said. "Ed and Neal wouldn't know him."

"We'd better find out," Clint said. "If he is here, at least it'll give us some idea of what this is all about."

"All these Texans coming here because of one man and what Tilghman did to him?" Bat asked.

"Phil Coe was one man in Abilene," Clint said, "and he had those Texans riled up enough to want to take on Bill Hickok."

"I guess you're right," Bat said. "When we relieve Ed and Neal I'll tell Ed to have Tilghman check and see if Texas Bill came into town."

"If he did he's going to stay undercover so you or Bill don't see him . . . until he's ready to be seen."

"Bill will find out," Bat said.

"Well, if he does I hope he holds on to his temper."

"He's been pretty low-key since the incident with Wes Hardin," Bat pointed out. "I think maybe that was what he needed."

"I hope you're right."

"I saw you sending smoke signals to Wyatt the other day," Bat said. "Why'd you want Tilghman in the Long Branch with you?"

"To keep my eye on him."

"You won't have to watch out for him once the action starts," Bat said.

"I didn't say I was going to watch out for him," Clint said. "I'll be too busy watching out for myself. No, I just want to keep my eye on him and make sure he doesn't start the action before we're ready."

"Think you can get him to follow your lead?"

"I hope so, Bat," Clint said. "I don't exactly like the idea of getting killed just because he's in a hurry to."

"I don't think you'll have to worry about that, Clint," Bat said, sincerely.

"I hope you're right, pal," Clint said. "For all our sakes, I hope you're right."

Chapter Thirty-Nine

During Clint and Bat's shift Clint saw Tilghman come down the street and stop by Bat, then cross over to his side.

"What's up?" Clint asked.

"Texas Bill didn't come in during the night," Tilghman said.

"I see," Clint said. "I can't believe that he'll come riding in in broad daylight and allow himself to be recognized."

"Maybe he's not involved in this," Tilghman suggested. "Maybe this is just a gang of men who are out to make a name for themselves. Dodge has quite a reputation, you know."

"I know."

"So, maybe they want to be known as the men who tore up Dodge City."

"That's a possibility," Clint admitted.

Tilghman remained quiet for a few moments, and then

broke the silence just seconds before Clint was going to. "Why'd you want me in the Long Branch with you?" he asked. Clint frowned, and the deputy went on, "I saw you giving signals to Wyatt when he was divvying up the saloons."

"Oh."

"You want to keep an eye on me? Is that it?"

Clint wondered how he would be able to put it so that the young man wouldn't take offense.

"Look," Tilghman said, before Clint could make a decision. "I admit, maybe I've been acting like a horse's ass, and maybe I've got a lot to learn."

Clint was surprised.

"I just want you to know that when the time comes, I'll follow your lead."

Clint studied the young deputy for a few moments and decided that he was sincere. "I appreciate that, Bill."

"Yeah, well, I appreciate you not badmouthing me to the marshal," Tilghman said. "You could have."

"No need," Clint said. "You're proving that right now."

Tilghman looked at Clint, then grinned and said, "Yeah, I guess maybe I am."

Clint had not seen Tilghman smile, or even grin, during his stay in Dodge, and it made the deputy look even younger than he was.

"We'll make out okay, kid," he said. "You better get over to the Long Branch. I think it's going to happen today."

Tilghman wet his lips and said, "I guess if you walk into the saloon in the next couple of hours, I'll know it's time."

"I don't think we'll even take a relief today, Bill. One

more group rides in, and I think it'll happen tonight.''

"Well, I'm ready," Tilghman said. He noticed Clint's quick look and added, "I said ready, not eager."

"Okay," the Gunsmith said.

He watched Tilghman cross the street and head for the Long Branch. It felt good to know that he had been right about the youngster. Given time, he'd make an excellent lawman. A few more years and he'd have the good judgment and the patience to go along with all of the other more natural tools that he already possessed.

He thought a little about himself, Wild Bill, Buckskin Frank Leslie. They all had reputations that were associated with their nicknames. At this point, Wyatt Earp, Bat Masterson and Bill Tilghman did not have nicknames, just their own names, and maybe that would make things easier for them. Reputations spread faster when they rode on a nickname for some reason. Bear River Tom Smith, the lawman in Abilene right before Wild Bill Hickok, was another example. Why, he'd even heard word of a young killer in New Mexico called Billy the Kid.

He hoped that Wyatt and Bat especially, since they were good friends of his, never allowed themselves to be christened with some outrageous alias by some ambitious newspaperman, as had been the case with him.

The Gunsmith! How much easier or different might his life have been if he had gone through as just plain Clint Adams, lawman. How many times had some young gunhawk come into a town where he was the law, looking to take on the Gunsmith, without even realizing that he was also the law in town? How many times had he been forced to kill in self-defense, thereby adding fuel to his own unwanted rep?

These boys were young, he thought, looking across the

street at Bat, and they had good, full lives ahead of them.

He remembered a line he had read back East once, about a rose being a rose no matter what you called it.

It was too bad that the same didn't hold true for people.

It was virtually impossible for him to separate ''the Gunsmith'' from Clint Adams, and only he knew that they were not necessarily the same person. In fact, the Gunsmith, as most people conceived him to be, did not exist at all.

Clint and Bat's shift was almost over when four more men rode into town. Once again they sank into the shadows of nearby doorways, and when the men passed and continued onto the livery, Clint trotted across the street to Bat.

''All right,'' he said. ''That makes fifteen. We've got to get set up now, Bat.''

''What if more come in?''

''We'll just have to be prepared for at least fifteen,'' Clint said. ''But maybe we'll get lucky and they'll split evenly with five going to each saloon.''

''The odds don't sound so bad that way.''

''I know they don't. Look, see if you can find Bassett in his office, and then you get over to the Alamo. I'll stop at the Alhambra and let Wyatt and Neal know. After that, we'll just have to stay in the saloons until they decide to make their move.''

Bat started away, and then stopped short.

''What's the matter?'' Clint asked.

''I just had a terrible thought,'' Bat said.

''What?''

''What happens if, while we're all in the saloons, they decide to hit the bank?''

"You didn't want to be a deputy sheriff in Dodge City forever, did you?"

Within fifteen minutes of those four men riding into town, everyone was set up.

Clint Adams and Bill Tilghman were in the Long Branch. Clint was standing by the bar, and Tilghman was standing at the roulette wheel table to the right of the front doors. Ben Thompson stood behind his faro table, apparently oblivious to everything but the cards he was dealing and the chips he was raking in.

At the Alamo, Bat Masterson had settled in at a corner poker game, seated so that he was able to watch the entire room, and his brother Ed was standing at the bar.

Over in the Alhambra, Wyatt Earp had taken up position on a platform that was raised fifteen feet above floor level, giving him a clear view of the entire room, including the front and back doors. Charlie Bassett was seated at a back table with a bottle of whiskey, seemingly slumped over in a drunken stupor. Neal Brown was standing at the bar nursing a beer.

The seven men who made up what could have been called "The Dodge City Gang" were in position and ready for anything that came their way.

Chapter Forty

The Alamo

Bat Masterson was not paying attention to the poker game that he was playing in, but he was cleaning up, nevertheless.

"I never seen such luck," one player remarked.

"Luck has nothing to do with it, my friend," Bat said, his attention on the front entrance of the saloon rather than on the man he was talking to.

As the cards were raked in and prepared for another deal, the batwing doors swung inward and several men walked through. *One*, Bat counted; *two, three, four. Yeah, there are five of them.* They hadn't ridden into town together, but now that they were here, they were seemingly throwing caution to the wind.

Bat caught his brother's eye, and Ed nodded, signifying that he was ready. Both men had removed their badges and pocketed them, so as not to spook the Texans.

As the five men entered the saloon, they split into three groups. Two men approached the bar, two went to a faro table, and the fifth man approached the poker table where Bat was playing, because there was an open chair.

"Mind if I sit in?" he asked.

"Help yourself, friend," Bat said. "The more the merrier, I always say."

Bat had no doubt that, somehow, the two at the bar, the two at the faro table, or the one sitting with him now would find a way to start trouble. It wasn't hard in a saloon. At the bar, perhaps, the men would claim that the drinks were watered down. At the faro table, they wouldn't like the deal, and here at the poker table, maybe the stranger would take offense at Bat's luck.

It remained to be seen.

Fifteen minutes went by, and the man at the table kept checking his pocket watch. Bat was starting to think that they had the whole thing timed to start trouble in all three saloons at the same time. If that was the case, there was going to be a hell of a lot of noise in Dodge in a very short time.

Soon, Bat knew that the trouble would start at his table, because the stranger began making comments, and was aiming them all at Bat himself.

"A little young to be in a place like this, ain't you?" the man said at one point.

"I go where the money is," Bat answered.

A little while later the man said, "Ain't it almost time for you to go to bed, sonny?"

"Not while you still got money on your side of the table, friend," Bat said.

And then, finally, the man said, "You know, boy, luck like yours is just too good to be true . . . or honest."

These were words designed to start trouble and, under normal circumstances, they would have. Bat, however, had decided to give the man a hard time.

"If you don't like the game, mister, there are others in town," he said.

"But I like this game," the man said, frowning. "It's you I don't like."

"Well, I'm sorry about that," Bat said, "but seems I heard it said someplace that you can't always satisfy everybody."

The man took a quick look at his watch, then pocketed it and frowned even more at Bat.

"You're thick-skinned, ain't you?"

"Helps in the winter."

"I'm saying you're a cheater!" the man shouted then, standing up so fast he knocked over his chair.

"Is that a fact?" Bat said, glancing lazily at the man.

"And yalla, too!"

"Are you trying to tell me that I appear jaundiced?" Bat asked, holding up his left hand to examine it. "Maybe I should go and see a doctor."

The man finally lost all patience and shouted, "Maybe you should go see the undertaker."

As the man went for his gun Bat fired his, which he had taken out long ago and held in his hand beneath the table. His bullet traveled up through the table and struck the man in the chest. The other players at the table all reeled over backwards to get out of the way of flying lead, and then scrambled to get to the door.

At the bar Ed Masterson had his eyes on the two Texans who had settled in there, and as they went for their guns he shouted, "Hey!"

The two men, attracted by the sound of his voice, looked his way with their hands halfway to their guns.

"Keep them leathered," Ed advised, but neither man was inclined to follow his advice. They both continued their moves toward their guns, and Ed Masterson drew his and fired twice. One man's hand never reached his gun as he slumped to the floor, the second man's fingertips had touched his, but that was as far as he got before he too fell to the floor. Both men were dead when they hit.

Meanwhile, Bat had stood up with his gun in his hand, keeping an eye on the two men at the faro table. They had been watching the action at the bar, and since Ed Masterson's back was to them, they decided that he was an easy mark.

Bat watched as both men drew their guns to shoot his brother in the back, and he fired as he shouted, "Ed!"

Ed spun, and as he did he fell to one knee. Both Masterson brothers fired at the two men, their bullets landing from opposite directions. The impact of their slugs cancelled each other out, and both men simply stood up straight and then slid to the floor, their guns dropping from their lifeless hands.

"Jesus!" the faro dealer screamed, and he fell over his table, as if trying to protect the felt from any flying drops of blood.

All five men who had entered were dead, and the Masterson brothers scanned the room quickly, lest there be a sixth hidden in among the crowd.

"That's all of them," Bat said, and Ed nodded.

In the sudden silence both men suddenly became aware of the sounds of gunfire from outside. It was clear that the action had also started at the Alhambra and the Long Branch.

"Let's go," Bat shouted, and both he and Ed ran from the Alamo to see if their help was needed elsewhere.

Chapter Forty-One

The Alhambra

Wyatt Earp sat on his platform with a twelve-gauge shotgun resting comfortably across his knees. Across the floor he could see Neal Brown sipping his beer and grimacing after each sip. If the man didn't like beer, he shouldn't try to drink it. He'd told him that time and time again.

From the corner of his eye Wyatt could see Charlie Bassett, who hadn't seemed to move a muscle since they got there. He hoped the man hadn't really gotten drunk and passed out.

He was in the act of lighting a cigarette when he saw the batwing doors swing open, and the men stepped in.

As Bat had done in the Alamo, Wyatt counted, and the count ended when he got to six. They were all dressed in trail clothes and were unshaven, and as they entered they broke off into three groupings of two.

166

He watched as two of them approached the bar, not far from where Neal was standing, and then two walked over to one of the house tables and started to watch the action.

Where had the other two—ah, there they were, and Wyatt almost started laughing. The other two had actually gone and sat at the same table with Charlie Bassett! He watched as one of the men spoke to Charlie, then nudged him, and when he got no response he plucked the whisky bottle from Charlie's seemingly nerveless fingers and passed it to his friend.

Briefly, Wyatt caught Neal's eye and the deputy nodded. It was only a matter of time now before they found some reason to start a ruckus.

As he continued to observe them he saw one of the men at the table with Charlie repeatedly check his watch. *They've got this thing timed,* he thought.

When one of the men standing at the house table suddenly walked away Wyatt frowned, but it soon became apparent where he was going. Obviously, they had spotted Wyatt sitting up on the platform and although Wyatt, Neal and Charlie had removed their badges, the men had decided to be cautious with the one man they could see might cause them some trouble. So, the lone man broke away from his friend and walked to the table directly beneath Wyatt's platform, where the marshal couldn't see him. Wyatt Earp would have to count on either Neal Brown or Charlie Bassett to keep that man from firing up through the platform and killing him.

The man who was left at the gaming table suddenly decided that this was where the trouble was slated to start. The man made a couple of plays, and then spoke to the dealer. The dealer replied, and suddenly the man shouted something, stepped back and went for his gun.

"Neal!" Wyatt Earp shouted, and at the same time he sprang from his chair and kicked it aside so that it fell to the floor below and broke into little pieces. He flattened himself against the wall with the shotgun against his chest and sure enough, the man beneath him began to fire through the platform. Chunks of wood flew up from two and then three holes in the platform floor, and then he heard the man beneath him cry out. Without waiting for confirmation that the man was hit he took two steps forward and leaped down from the platform. He landed on a table, which splintered beneath his weight, and he rolled with the force of the fall to avoid injury. As he came up to one knee he saw the two men at the bar bearing down on Neal Brown, who had apparently not only fired at the man beneath the platform, but the one at the gaming table who had started the action. Wyatt leveled the shotgun and fired both barrels at the two men. As the double-aught load smacked into both men they were spun around, their revolvers flying from their hands and striking the mirror behind the bar. As they slumped to the floor, both Neal Brown and Wyatt Earp turned their attention to the corner table where Charlie Bassett had been sitting.

Bassett had not merely been playing possum at that table, but while sitting slumped over had been cradling his .45 in his lap. When he heard Wyatt Earp shout out to Neal Brown, he wasted no time. He fired through the table top at the man on his left, and the bullet entered beneath the man's chin and exited from the top of his head, taking most of the head with it.

Immediately as he fired Bassett threw his weight to his left, toppling his chair and by doing so saved his life. The man on his right had fired by this time, but the slug slammed harmlessly into the wall behind where Bassett's head had been moments before. From the floor Bassett fired again, and this time his slug took the second man high in the chest, knocking him and his chair over backwards.

The shooting was over, and whatever customers had not fled from the saloon were either lying on the floor or crouched under tables.

"That it?" Bassett shouted, pushing himself up from the floor.

Wyatt and Neal had been looking around the room, waiting for someone to throw in with the six men, but when no one appeared inclined to do so, Wyatt said, "That's it!"

A few moments later, Bat and Ed Masterson came running through the front door, guns ready, and all five men barely avoided shooting each other.

"Is it over?" Bat asked.

They all became aware of the gunfire coming from the Long Branch down the block, and as Wyatt Earp replied, "Not quite!" they all ran out of the Alhambra and toward the Long Branch.

Chapter Forty-Two

The Long Branch

Clint alternated his gaze for the sake of variety, first watching the door, then Bill Tilghman, and finally Ben Thompson before returning his eyes to the door.

Tilghman seemed a bit nervous, but you couldn't really see it unless you looked closely. He would clench and unclench his hands, and do the same with the muscles in his jaw, but since he was standing by the roulette wheel, his nervous moves, if noticed, could have been put down to gambling—unless you also noticed that he wasn't playing, but simply standing by the table.

Ben Thompson always seemed intent on his dealing, never looking up while Clint was looking at him. Clint made a game of it at one point, looking at the door, then skipping Tilghman and looking right at Thompson to see if he could catch him looking up, but no matter how he varied his gaze, he never caught Thompson looking at anything but the cards.

Clint had ordered a beer when he reached the bar and, like Neal Brown, he was nursing it—though not for the same reason. The Gunsmith liked beer quite a lot, but he drank very sparingly while playing cards, and even less when he was in a situation that might call for gunplay.

Such as this one.

As nervous as he knew Tilghman must be—in spite of what Bat thought about his fellow deputy—that's how calm the Gunsmith felt. Calm or not, however, he still didn't like the implication of what happened next.

He was watching the batwing doors when suddenly they swung inward to admit the Texans.

Counting, Clint was quite surprised when he had to go beyond five to six . . . *seven* . . . *and eight* . . .

We miscalculated, he thought. They'd been geared for at least fifteen, but the Texans wouldn't be sending half that number into one saloon. What if they had sent eight into each place? Two against eight were mighty bad odds, no matter what kind of a reputation you had.

Clint had never really believed that there would be more than a dozen men, fifteen at the outside. Adjustments were going to have to be made now, and he hoped that the others would be able to make them. Wyatt would have the best chance, because he had both Neal Brown and Charlie Bassett, but what about the Mastersons? They were alone at the Alamo.

Here, Clint had Tilghman and himself. Thompson was there, of course, but it remained to be seen how active a part he was intending to take in the proceedings.

Clint caught Tilghman's eye and the young deputy nodded, though it was plain that he was feeling some apprehension, as well. A look at Thompson revealed nothing different. He was intent on dealing his game.

As the eight men entered, obviously unconcerned about anyone seeing them together, two of them walked straight ahead and took up positions at Thompson's table, three of them headed to the bar, and the others went to an empty table and sat down. They had attracted some attention when they entered, but gradually people were going back to what they were doing, and in moments the men were forgotten—by everyone but Tilghman and Clint.

Clint and Tilghman had already worked out a plan of their own. Since the three men sitting at the table were on the deputy's side of the room, they were to be his responsibility. Clint would have to split his attention between the three men at the bar, and the two at the faro table. He started to wish that he had taken his Springfield with him. It was a measure of overconfidence that he hadn't, and that bothered him. He had always been confident of his abilities, but overconfidence could be deadly.

He called the bartender over and asked, ''What kind of a weapon do you have behind the bar?''

The bartender looked nervous and said, ''Uh, a shotgun.''

''Double barrel?''

''Yeah.''

''Where is it?''

''In the center of the bar.''

''Without making a big show out of it, slide it to this end of the bar and put it right below my beer mug. Understand?''

''Yes, sir.''

Mopping the bar with a rag, the bartender worked his way to the center of the bar, and worked his way back, and when he finished the shotgun was in place.

"Is there gonna be some shooting?" he asked Clint, nervously.

"A lot of shooting," Clint said. "You just get ready to hit the deck."

"Yes, sir."

The three men who were drinking at the bar were standing at the end furthest away from Clint. Closer to him were the two men at the faro table.

"Bartender," one of the men called.

"Yes?"

"What do you call this?" the man asked, holding up a bottle of whiskey.

"Uh, that's whiskey, friend," the barkeep answered.

"Whiskey?" the man said. Looking at one of his friends he asked, "Does that taste like whiskey to you?"

"Not to me," the man replied.

With that the man holding the bottle threw it toward the bartender, who didn't know that the man had deliberately thrown high. The bartender ducked and the bottle flew way over his head and smashed into the bottles behind the bar.

"Get me and my friends some real whiskey!" the man shouted.

"Excuse me," Clint called out. He hoped that Tilghman was watching his men instead of what was going on at the bar.

"You talking to us, friend?" the man asked.

"That's right, I'm talking to you."

"What have you got to say?"

"Well, I was just thinking that if you boys don't like the whiskey here, there are plenty of other saloons in town."

"Hell, mister," the man said, "we like this place just fine, it's just the whiskey we don't like."

"Then drink the beer," Clint suggested.

"We're whiskey drinkers," the man said. "Beer is for lily-livered jaspers like you."

"Is that a fact?"

"That's a fact," the man confirmed.

"I've got a better idea now," Clint said. He was reaching into his shirt pocket as he spoke, and as he said, "Why don't you and your friends saddle up and leave town," he pinned Bill Tilghman's badge on his shirt. He had taken it from Tilghman earlier, thinking that it might come in handy later. If he was hoping the men would pause at the sight of the badge, though, he had been wrong. If anything, it made them more eager to go for their guns.

"Hey, boys, look who's a lawman," the first man said. "I been going to put some holes in a lawman ever since we left Texas."

When the man looked away from Clint, he knew what was coming next. The man had turned his head hoping to catch Clint off guard, but as he drew his gun, the Gunsmith jumped up and rolled backward over the bar, dropping down on the other side just as the three men fired. When the three of them realized what had happened, they attempted to correct their aim, but by the time they could Clint had snatched up the shotgun and fired both barrels at them.

The shot spread as it flew towards the men, and it smacked into all three of them. The only thing was, it wasn't buckshot, it was birdshot!

"Christ!" one of the men shouted as it hit him, and then the three of them were staring down at their bloodstained shirts, wondering why they hadn't been torn apart.

"Birdshot," one of them yelled, and then they started to raise their guns again.

At the same time, the three men sitting at the empty table started to stand up in order to reach their guns, but

Tilghman didn't give them a chance. The table being in the way of their draw gave him the extra edge he needed. He drew and fired, catching the first man as he was clearing his chair. The other two men saw their comrade fall, and turned towards Tilghman just as he fired again. His shot caught the second man in the belly and knocked him back, and as the third man cleared leather and raised his gun Tilghman crouched and fired again. His gun punched the man in the throat, just below the chin, and then took the back of his head with him as it exited.

Clint discarded his borrowed shotgun and in one fluid, graceful motion drew his gun. The three men were slow in throwing off the shock of the birdshot, and as they raised their guns the Gunsmith was already firing. With his modified, double-action revolver, there was no need for him to cock the hammer before he pulled the trigger, so he simply yanked his finger back three times, striking each man in the chest right above the heart.

That done, the Gunsmith quickly turned his attention to the men at the faro table, as did young Bill Tilghman, but they were already reeling back from the impact of two well-placed shots from Ben Thompson's .45.

At that same moment, Wyatt Earp and the rest of the lawmen of Dodge came barreling through the batwing doors, almost tripping over some of the patrons who had hit the deck at the first sign of lead.

The gunsmoke floated towards the ceiling of the deathly quiet room, like a fine, white mist.

"Everybody okay?" Clint asked.

They all looked at each other, as if no one had really thought to check themselves for wounds, and when the inventory had been taken, Wyatt said, "Everybody seems to be okay."

He approached Clint at the bar while the rest of them

walked around, checking bodies.

"How many?" he asked Clint.

"Eight," Clint said. "How about you?"

"We had six," Wyatt said. He turned to Bat and asked him the same question.

"Five," Bat said. "All dead."

"That makes nineteen," Clint said. "We missed four somehow when they came in."

"Let's just be glad we didn't miss them now," Wyatt said.

"We might have," Clint said, "if it hadn't been for Ben."

They all turned their gazes toward Ben Thompson, who stood behind his faro table, appearing quite amused by the sudden attention.

Raising the gun in his hand, which was his Colt Frontier model .45 and not the light Cloverleaf he had been wearing, he said, "I told you I'd wear a larger gun, next time."

Chapter Forty-Three

Word got around pretty quick that Dodge City had been invaded by a band of Texans, with the numbers varying from twenty to fifty to a hundred, who had all been killed by eight men. Newspapers were calling the Gunsmith, Ben Thompson, Wyatt Earp, Bat Masterson, Ed Masterson, Bill Tilghman, Charlie Bassett, and Neal Brown "The Dodge City Gang."

"Quite a nickname, huh?" Wyatt asked, showing Clint the newspaper article.

Clint regarded the newspaper with distaste. His only good thought was that at least they had not gone and christened each man separately. Lumped together like that, the all-encompassing nickname would not do anyone too much harm.

Of course, the biggest play in the newspapers went to the legendary Gunsmith, who, it said, had singlehandedly disposed of at least ten men.

"By eyewitness account," Wyatt finished reading.

"This eyewitness must have had four eyes and he was seeing double in all of them."

"I'd like to give him four black eyes," Clint said, "if I ever find out who he is."

"The Dodge City Gang, huh?" Neal Brown asked, looking over their shoulders. "That's some name, huh?"

"Don't let it go to your head," Clint advised.

"Oh, no," Neal said. "Everytime it does I'll just think back to how scared I was in that saloon."

They were all in Wyatt Earp's office—with the exception of Charlie Bassett, who was in *his* office—and Wyatt gave Neal the newspaper to pass around.

"I wonder how those extra four got into town without us seeing them?" Bill Tilghman said aloud.

"I guess we'll just have to be grateful that it was only four more," Clint said.

"You said it," Tilghman agreed. "Boy, when those eight men walked in . . ." He shook his head.

"Well, it's over now," Wyatt said.

"What are you going to do now, Wyatt?" Clint asked. "Stay on as marshal?"

"I thought I'd see what it was like to be a deputy marshal for a while, before I move on," Wyatt said.

"Who's going to be marshal?"

"Ed there wants to try it out," Wyatt said. "Let him shoulder the responsibility for a while."

"What about you, Bat?" Clint asked.

"I've sort of been toying with the idea of running against Charlie in the upcoming election," Bat said. "I think I'd make a pretty good sheriff."

"I think so too," Clint said. He looked at Tilghman then and said, "Bill?"

"I'll stick around and be a deputy for a while," he said,

"whether it be for Charlie or Bat. Either way, I've still got a lot to learn, and I might as well learn it right here."

"Good move," Clint said. "I guess you'll have Ben Thompson to contend with for a while, at least until he puts a bankroll together."

"What about you?" Bat asked.

"Me," Clint said, "I'll head back to Labyrinth, Texas, pick up my rig and be on the move again." He stood up to leave and told them, "If you fellas ever need me for anything, though, drop me a line in Labyrinth. I'll be in and out of there."

"We'll get together again, Clint," Wyatt said. "Don't worry."

"Sure," Bat agreed. "The Dodge City Gang rides again."

"Okay," Clint said, grinning, "but next time, let's make it for a poker game, huh?"

Author's Note

This novel is based on certain historical facts.

Bat Masterson and *Bill Tilghman* actually were deputy sheriffs in Dodge City for a while, during 1875 and 1876. Bat went on to be elected sheriff in 1877, and Tilghman served under him as a deputy.

Wyatt Earp and *Neal Brown* did, in fact, respond to a call for help from Mayor George Hoover in 1876, for the reasons stated in the book. There are conflicting reports that Earp was appointed marshal, or deputy marshal. *Ed Masterson* also arrived with them.

Charlie Bassett was sheriff during the time period in which this story takes place.

Clay Allison did reportedly come to Dodge City and was wounded in a gun battle with Bill Tilghman.

Ben Thompson did work as a dealer in the Long Branch Saloon.

John Wesley Hardin did at one time or another pass through Dodge City.

All of these historical characters are brought together in this book through poetic license. There is no evidence, however, that they had all ever come together in Dodge City at the same time.

If they had, though, the Gunsmith was sure to have been there too.

GREAT BOOKS

E-BOOKS

AUDIOBOOKS

& MORE

Visit us today

www.speakingvolumes.us

Made in the USA
Las Vegas, NV
25 February 2021

18615653R00111